TAPESTRY OF SHADOWS AND LIGHT

THE HUNTERS - PREQUEL

RORI BLEU

ROSIE CHAPEL

First printing: 2025
ISBN: 978-1-7637753-2-9 (ebook)
ISBN: 978-1-7637753-3-6 (paperback)

Ulfire Pty. Ltd.
P.O. Box 1481
South Perth
WA 6951
Australia

Cover Design: Rebecca Norman
Images Courtesy: Canva.
Designed in Canva using appropriate licences.

❀ Formatted with Vellum

1

Fuelled by the news blackout from the other side of the Atlantic, rendering citizens defenceless against the looming annihilation of humanity, protests erupted across Europe.

The once peaceful demonstrations had descended into anarchy, triggered by rumours about the soaring death toll, exacerbated by the loudly touted, mandated, and hastily administered miracle inoculations — given the cure seemed no less deadly than the disease.

Even Rome… the Eternal City… was not spared.

The drum of thousands of marching feet, along with chants of "Stop the Lies" and "Murderers", filled the night air. Burning cars and torched storefronts illuminated the widening chaos, as the masses demanded their leaders release any and all vaccines immediately, to halt the spread of the mysterious plague and help those in need.

Without warning, those who had congregated in the Piazza Venezia switched their focus, sending a wave of humanity towards the barricade of police and soldiers blocking off the Via del Corso. Their target — the Palazzo

Chigi, seat of Italian power, and the perceived corruption therein.

Armed with makeshift clubs, the front line of protesters, young and old alike, battered those facing them dressed in the military-issued riot gear.

Clouds of green, white, and red spray paint floated across the cordon in a concerted effort to obscure the vision of those behind the visors, to blind them to the barrage of rocks and bricks being hurled at them from the rear. Wild hands snatched out in a violent rage, trying to rid the defenders of their helmets.

Control slipping, a signal from behind the barriers unleashed the army's water cannons.

The deluge knocked victims from both sides off their feet, reducing them to mangled heaps. Too many, caught underfoot by others scrambling to avoid the pounding water, were crushed to death in the melee.

Despite the bleeding gash to his head, a souvenir of one of the brick throwers, Colonnello Giulio Ricci avoided the stampede by slithering under an IVECO Puma. Fortunately, the six-wheeled behemoth had proved too heavy for the mob to overturn, but the odour of burning petrol indicated that a Molotov cocktail had found its way to the upper portion of the armoured fighting vehicle.

Ricci felt hands grab him from behind. Instinctively, he lashed out at the culprit.

"Whoa, Colonnello, it is me, Tenente Lombardy," the medic exclaimed as he dodged the blow.

Trying to elicit a chuckle from the ailing officer, Lombardy added, "And before you try to pummel me to death, sir, at least allow me to check you out so it's a fair fight."

Lombardy examined the colonel, especially his pupils which were slow to react under the flashlight.

Not happy with the results, Lombardy clicked off the light. "Looks like whatever bounced off your head left you with more than a nasty cut. I am guessing you probably have a concussion. I'll organise an ambulance to transport you to the base hosp—"

Ricci's raised palm stopped Lombardy's evaluation. "Never mind me. Get the injured to hospitals and medical centres with an armed escort in case any of the administrators see fit to balk at my directives."

"B-but Colonnello Ricci, what about you? That's a bad cut. I need to make sure you are not suffering from a more severe trauma," the medic protested.

"Bah… do not waste your time on me. My wife is more than capable of stitching me back together. Now, do as I say."

Reluctantly, Lombardy acquiesced, and threw his superior officer a half-hearted salute, knowing it was a mistake to leave him unattended.

Orders were orders.

As the last drops of adrenaline drained from his body, Ricci registered the pounding in his skull was increasing in direct proportion with his fading consciousness.

Seeking out his second-in-command, Ricci found Maggiore Viscuso attempting to secure the barriers. The Sicilian major was barking instructions to his subordinates when Ricci clasped his shoulder, more to steady himself than to get Viscuso's attention.

Spinning on his heel, Viscuso snatched Ricci before the latter hit the ground.

As observant as the medic, Viscuso was perturbed by the amount of blood dripping down Ricci's face. Cognizant that head wounds bleed more copiously than other areas of the body, did not stop him summoning one of the corpsmen to tend to Ricci.

"No, Maggiore, save your breath. While there is a respite from the protests, rebuild the barricades and see to the defence of the Palazzo. We cannot afford to let the rabble beyond this point."

"Aye, sir, but at least allow me to assign someone to see you to the base hospital."

"No, Edoardo—" The two men had served together for nearly two decades, making the usual formalities meaningless under the circumstances. "—if you can spare a driver to take me home, Noemi will patch me up. I'll be back before you know I'm gone."

"Giulio, knowing your wife, I doubt she'll send you anywhere except an early grave if you even think of coming back," Viscuso tried to convince his friend. "Rest up. Tomorrow will be here soon enough bringing with it another push, requiring your expertise."

Ricci nodded in agreement, compounding the throbbing in his head.

"Hey, you there. I need your assistance," the major hailed a nearby police constable.

The constable spun on his heel, pointed to himself to verify he was indeed the man being addressed, while shooting Viscuso an incredulous glare at being summoned in so discourteous a manner.

Viscuso groused, "Yes, you, you ass. Escort my commanding officer home and see he does not return this evening."

Rather than argue, the constable considered it a blessing from the heavens to play nursemaid to an obviously high-ranking officer, rather than face the vindictive hordes rampaging through the city. "Right away, sir," he agreed genially.

Stepping closer to the two men, the policeman hefted Ricci from Viscuso's shoulder to his, and then aided the injured colonel to his patrol car.

By the time the car crossed into Trastevere, Ricci's headache was so severe his eyesight had blurred but, unwilling to worry Noemi, decided not to mention it.

Parking in front of the colonel's home, the constable hurried around the vehicle to assist the soldier from the backseat, offering to help him to the door.

Ricci waved him off. "I am not an old woman," he growled. "Thank you for your help, but you'd best get back to the piazza quick smart. You're no use to them here."

The constable was about to remind the injured colonel about Viscuso's edict, but Ricci was already at the door.

"Fucking, soldiers," the younger man muttered under his breath. "They all think they are some kind of national hero."

Watching Ricci lean against the glass panel, fumbling with his keys, the constable took pity on him, followed him to the door, rang the bell, and was back in his vehicle, before Ricci could complain about him ignoring orders.

Pebbles spun out from under the from under the car's tyres as he accelerated away, then the street fell quiet again.

In contrast with the heated voices coming from within the Ricci's house. The loudest, of course, being that of his wife… and it was approaching the entrance.

"That's what I am saying. That vaccine was released in America untested because Worthington wanted to be the first on the market so his company could win the NIH's contracts. He might as well have filled their veins with rat poison.

"On the other hand, if we had been given time and resources to run proper experimentation on *ours*—"

What she was about to say changed abruptly when she yanked open the door. "Goddammit, Giulio, I just got a call from Edoardo. Why didn't you let him take you—"

Giulio's ungainly stumble into Noemi's arms, interrupted her admonishment.

The handful of people seated at the Ricci's dining room turned to see Noemi struggling to prevent her husband from collapsing.

"Lorenzo, Francesco," she yelled to her fellow researchers, gathered at her home for dinner and discussion. "Help me get Giulio to the table. Chiara, grab the first-aid kit from under the sink in the bathroom."

No one needed to be told twice.

Carefully, the men assisted Ricci, to the table, the arms of the chair they settled him into holding him upright... after a fashion.

Chiara returned with a medical bag, and set it in front of Noemi who was already examining her husband's injury, chastising him for being bull-headed enough to refuse proper care.

"Like I told that mother hen Viscuso, I just need you to patch me up and I'll be fine. I must get back as quickly as possible."

"Not bloody likely," Noemi retorted. "You have two daughters who need you more than those self-important peacocks at the Military Hospital." Sniffing back a sob, she whispered, "Not to mention your wife."

His head hurt too much to argue, and he made do with a reassuring, "I was at the Chigi," he felt the need to clarify, as though that made any difference in the overall scheme of things, "...and don't worry, mí amore, I'm fine."

"I thought you were assigned to defend the Military Hospital from looters?" Noemi paused to level an inquisitive gaze at her husband.

Waiting for her to work her magic with a suture or two, he said, "I was, but they needed more support at the palace. Total chaos it is." He heaved a weary sigh. "If you can get me a glass of water and a couple of aspirin, I'll sit here for a while and let you lot get back to your discussion."

Noemi sent him a strange glance. It was not normal for Giulio to ask for aspirin... or any medication for that matter. He was paranoid about becoming addicted. He had seen it take its toll on his father.

She fetched a pitcher of water and a glass from the kitchen, then sank into the chair opposite to keep an eye on him.

The others returned to the subject causing them the greatest concern.

"I tell you, Noemi," Francesco said in no uncertain terms, "it's time to cut our losses and flee the city before it is too late."

In her Italianised Bostonian accent, Chiara was quick to agree. "He's right, boss. The Americans failed to identify the plague, let alone secure a cure for it. As for us, we have only broken it down partially, but nothing we've tried eradicates it completely.

"My cousin in Belfast told me it's already reached the Irish shores and is wreaking havoc across the country and, as much as the Brits are trying to isolate themselves from the rest of the world, it will only take a stiff breeze. There's no way to close your borders to nature."

"But we've broken the code sequence. It's only a matter of time—"

"No, Noemi," Chiara interrupted. "I have my family to think about, and you…" waving at Giulio, "…should be more concerned about your own family than strangers who don't give a fig. Like you told your husband, you have two children who need you."

Noemi hated her words being flung back at her, but conceded she was on the losing end of the debate.

"And where do we run to?" she asked, sarcastically. "Australia?"

That made Giulio chuckle. "I have been trying to get you to take a vacation for years… and only now you think of traveling overseas?"

"Shush yourself, Giulio. You are just as guilty as I."

An unsteady hand reached for the pitcher of water, Giulio's fingers… no, the whole of his right arm… tingled to the point of numbness. He tried to push it aside, attempting to lift the inexplicably heavy pitcher from the table, irked because his ability to come up with a witty retort eluded him.

Verbally sparring with Noemi was always his pride and joy… not tonight.

Giulio's face blanched. His eyes widened in a fear he had never experienced before.

Desperately, he grappled for coherence to plead for help, only to have it dribble out of his mouth in incomprehensible babble.

The strength in his right arm gave way, and the glass pitcher crashed to the floor, sending shards and water splattering across the tiles.

The last thing Colonnello Giulio Ricci saw as he slumped to the side of his chair, the subarachnoid haemorrhage claiming his life, was his beloved Noemi knocking over her chair when she leapt out of it, screaming his name.

C hiara, after texting her husband to let him know what had happened, offered to watch over Noemi's sleeping daughters, while the other three conveyed Giulio to Noemi's Volkswagen, and set off in search of any medical facility not already flooded with the dead and dying.

It ought to have been a simple mission.

Not tonight.

Hours of trying proved futile.

No one had bargained for the brutal, almost instantaneous breakdown of society and Rome was left reeling.

Despondently, and amidst the blaring of sirens, they returned to Noemi's, laid Giulio on the sofa, and covered him with a blanket.

Thanking her friends for the help and exhorting them to flee the city immediately, Noemi collapsed in a chair and wept.

The drum of feet, heralding Bianca's approach, jolted Noemi awake. She was startled to realise, in her grief-fed exhaustion, she had dozed off.

"Papa, you terrible at hide and seek," the child carolled. "I show you how to play."

Her voice echoed along the corridor as she skipped away to her usual hiding place.

A fresh bout of tears brimmed over as Noemi's gaze swung from her happy daughter to the lifeless corpse which was once her husband.

How am I going to explain this to her when I cannot fathom it myself?

After what felt like an eternity, Noemi stifled her sobs, pledging, for the sake of her daughters, not to let them see any sign of weakness.

From today, I am both mama and papa. Tears will not help my children.

Noemi pulled her phone from her pocket to inform her office that, due to a family emergency, she would not be in for the next few days, taken aback when her mobile provider informed in a robotic drone, "Owing to the high volume of calls, the system is unable to connect you."

She tried several times during the next few minutes, receiving the same message every time, prompting her to check on the state of the city.

Turning on the television, she was appalled to see images of the blazing inferno, which was once the Palazzo Chigi, dominating every channel. Reports confirming the downfall of the government, were supported by scenes of an angry mob rampaging through the building, intent on obliterating any and all reminders of the abject failure of their erstwhile leaders, who had fled with judicious haste.

Eyewitness accounts of widespread vandalism and looting compounded the terror.

The news was interrupted by a blaring warning and the screen displayed an Emergency Message.

Sombrely, an automated voice declared, "Your attention please. This is not a test. The chief of the combined armed forces has issued a state of emergency. Martial law is now in effect. All residents are to remain in their homes until further notice. Further instructions will be issued shortly."

The television squealed its warning again, repeating the directive.

The sound of running feet prompted Noemi to switch off the television.

"Mama, mama what's that funny noise?" Bianca appeared at the doorway.

"It was just the television, poppet. Nothing to fret over."

Noemi's reply went over Bianca's head because she was more interested in why papa was still lying under the blanket.

"Papa, you were s'posed to come look for me, not keep sleepin' under there."

Taking a step closer, the little girl stretched out chubby fingers to twitch the sheet. "Stop playing ghost and make me your special pancakes."

Noemi caught her daughter's hand. "Papa had to play soldier until late last night. How about I make you breakfast, and we'll let papa sleep a little longer?"

"Will you put smiley faces on like papa does? 'Cos usually you don't."

Summoning up a weak smile, Noemi suggested, "How about I cook them, and *you* decorate them."

"Really?" This was the first time either mama or papa had suggested Bianca help cook. "I bet papa will wake up when he smells the yummy breakfast."

A loud rap propelled Noemi to the front door. Grabbing Giulio's service pistol, she peered through the sidelight to verify the identity of the caller.

She had fired the gun she now gripped once, nearly killing the neighbour's cat, after mistaking it for an intruder. Her appalling aim aside, bearing in mind society's apparent descent into mayhem, she had no intention of opening the door unarmed. Not today… or ever.

Recognising Chiara standing on the other side, she breathed a sigh of relief, and opened the door, to see her friend swinging an impatient gaze between the house and the Fiat 500 parked at the curb, engine idling.

"Thank God, you are here, Chiara."

Seeing a wide-eyed Chiara take a step back, Noemi opened her mouth to ask what was wrong, then realised she was still aiming the weapon at her friend.

Lowering her arm, Noemi blushed profusely and babbled an apology.

Chiara grumbled, "Whatever. I just wanted to let you know we're leaving, and you should come with us."

"Where on earth are you going?"

"Santino received orders from his base to report to an evac camp at the Port of Taranto immediately."

"Why, in God's name?"

"To oversee the *unpeopling* of healthy citizens from the peninsula to a refugee camp outside Tripoli. Evidently, gold is still considered a valuable commodity, and the Libyans are willing to open their desert for a select group of Italians to get their hands on it."

Unpeopling? What will they dream up next? Noemi gave vent to an internal eye roll. Stunned at this development, which sounded like the ravings of a lunatic mind, she tried to wrap her head around the ridiculous plan the army had formulated.

Would it not be more sensible to focus their energies on producing a reliable test for the pathogen, her research team had identified?

This crackpot notion meant only those refugees who were not dead, dying, or at least, running a fever, would be allowed to board a ship and transported to a godforsaken sand dune where they were likely to die of thirst or malnutrition for want of suitable infrastructure.

Images of displaced people, living in desperate circumstances in tent cities pestered her consciousness. It was not a pretty picture.

She doubted the Libyans intended to provide any further aid.

Never mind that, despite no official reports of the virus on the African continent, which *everyone* in the labs found ironic, the reliability of medical services there remained a serious concern.

The healthy were just as likely to face a medical ambush once they had arrived.

Noemi beseeched, "I know your husband is as wed to the military as was mine but, in this case, he needs to ignore the directive and take you all north."

"North?" Chiara parroted incredulously. "There's no protection for us in that direction."

Noemi, smacking the barrel of the gun against her palm, replied implacably, "We'll create our own."

Santino blared the horn, drawing Chiara's attention his way, surprised to see her husband out of the vehicle, waving furiously for her to get in the car so they could leave.

She had argued much the same thing with Santino before they left home. A nagging voice in her brain insisting it was a mistake to head south, but the uncertainty of what may lie to the north was no more reassuring.

Chiara was torn between loyalty to her husband who wanted to follow orders, and her own gut instinct which agreed with Noemi.

Her only qualm was the lack of protection if they went north. They had small children to consider, never mind their own safety, and whether she could persuade Santino that, for once, his superiors had made a huge mistake.

"You think it's better for us to head to the unknown, Noemi? Where exactly do you want to go?"

"For now, please take my girls with you. I am sure they can keep Nicoletta occupied. There's a resort on the outskirts of Settebagni in a renovated castello—"

"This is Italy. There's a castello in every town being used as a hotel, or a service station. Be more specific," Chiara sniped.

"Shut up and listen," Noemi snapped.

Taking a breath, she tried to calm herself, before she chased away her friend.

"It's on the northern edge of the city. Get a room there. I'll join you as soon as I can, and we'll plan our escape."

"Where exactly are *you* goin', boss?" Gone was Chiara's careful Italian. In its place, her clipped, Bostonian English.

"I need to attend to things here. Trust me, I'll be right behind you."

Giving Chiara no chance to protest, Noemi urged her inside to help get the girls ready.

Noemi drove across the eerily quiet Ponte Sublicio on her way to the English cemetery just off Via Marmorata, her mind reeling with the events of the morning... of the last twenty-four hours.

Yesterday, life was perhaps not normal exactly, but predictable. Giulio protected the citizens; she worked to develop an antidote to this catastrophic virus. In the blink of an eye, everything had changed, and her thoughts hurtled through her head like an out-of-control freight train.

She slapped the steering wheel in frustration. "How do we fix this mess, Giulio?" she demanded, refusing to grant tears the upper hand.

"I did not give you permission to leave me. We were supposed to grow old together, watch our kids get married. Have you *any* idea how to explain the death of a parent to their child... our child? I thought my heart would splinter. Praise the Gods that Sophia is too young to understand. Do not think dying on me gets you off the hook."

She gave a watery sniff.

Before Chiara's unexpected arrival on the doorstep, Noemi had steeled herself and, as gently as possible, explained to Bianca about her father, which almost undid her resolve not to weep in front of her daughter.

Bianca's expression of abject bewilderment, reared up in her vision.

As the truth left Noemi's lips, the little girl had stopped chewing her mouthful of pancake, her cheeks bulging like a chipmunk's storing food for winter. Finally, Bianca managed a hard swallow, striving to make sense of her mama's words.

After a shocked silence, Bianca, with the natural resilience innate to children, her voice wobbling and two fat tears rolling down her cheeks, had hugged her mother and said, "I'll look after you."

Her childish stoicism shattered something inside Noemi who sank to the floor with Bianca enveloped in her arms, and the two sobbed.

Bianca's practical reaction… unusual in one so young yet would be a trait she carried for life… proved cathartic. Noemi collected herself, organised breakfast and, while Bianca munched on questionably embellished pancakes, went to tend to Sophia who had slept through the entire crisis.

Noemi swung into the cemetery housing the Pyramid of Cestius and found a suitable place to park. No tourists wandering the peaceful graveyard today, checking out the resting places of Shelley and Keats, among others.

Getting Giulio there was one thing, working out where to bury him… quite another.

In a quiet corner, almost as if the caretakers were expecting an influx of bodies, Noemi noticed several graves already dug.

"Clearly, they have seen the news," she muttered.

Never one to look a gift horse in the mouth, she found a convenient trolley and, gritting her teeth, manoeuvred Giulio's body onto it — still encased in the blanket.

Behaving as though this was something she did every day, Noemi trundled along the path to the closest pit. Struggling, but determined, she did what she never thought she would have to do with as much dignity as possible.

Spying a shovel, she covered Giulio's remains with a layer of dark brown earth and murmured a few words of farewell. She took a modicum of comfort that he was in the company of luminaries such as the poets Percy Bysshe Shelly and John Keats, the famed Italian Marxist philosopher and politician, Antonio Gramsci, and the Norwegian historian, P A Munch. A handful of the historical figures he had so admired.

A soldier first, Giulio was also a well-educated man, and never stopped expanding his knowledge. One of the qualities they had in common.

Unwilling to leave her adored husband alone, Noemi stood for a long time, memories of their years together flooding her mind. The day they met, walking hand-in-hand along the Tiber, their wedding, the birth of their daughters. Passion, laughter, shared joys and sorrows… image after image chased across her vision.

In the reverent hush of the cemetery, Noemi thanked the stars, she had ignored tradition and taken her husband's name when they married, leaving her with another part of him, albeit intangible, forever.

Then, she turned her back on that chapter of her life and faced what she suspected would be a very challenging future.

3

———

Noemi had one last place to stop before she left the city, her laboratory in the bowels of Ringtonwoth Pharmaceuticals: Roma.

To her unease, the entrance was not manned, and the barrier raised. Her stomach knotted. Had looters already stormed the building and absconded with anything they could get their hands on?

She closed her eyes, imagining the ramifications of even a small percentage of the drugs the company manufactured falling into the wrong hands.

"*Stronzi,*" she hissed balefully. "Like we don't have enough shit to deal with."

Noemi cruised slowly up the drive, slowing her VW to a standstill at the sight of two shiny, black, government-type vehicles, complete with darkened windows, idling in front of the centre's massive front doors. Neither bore any official insignias and their plates were unfamiliar.

The only reason she did not turn tail and flee were the drugs she knew would be needed.

"Buck up, Ricci," Noemi growled as she tucked Giulio's

pistol into the waistband of her jeans, and twisted to shrug her small backpack over her shoulders. "This is your building. You gave a fancy speech to convince your friends to risk their lives by going with you. Time to prove you've got what it takes to be the type of leader who will keep them safe."

Switching off the engine, she alighted as quietly as possible, leaving the door ajar in case she had to make an emergency escape.

The neatly manicured lawn ruffled under her feet as, crossing the grass to avoid crunching along the gravel path, Noemi circled the building to the door at the rear which her identification card would unlock, the one adjacent to the Staff Room.

Pausing at the corner closest to said door, Noemi became one with the wall, withdrew the gun, and levelled it in front of her. Giulio had taught her to aim for the centre mass and, for God's sake, not to shoot herself in the foot. The near death of the neighbour's cat was more than enough to drive *that* point home.

She peeked around to check whether the coast was clear, surprised and relieved to note the entry stood unattended. Seemingly, whoever was inside had considered the usual influx of employees unlikely after the riots.

A second fact occurred to Noemi, which played in her favour. This compound was off-grid and, thus, not dependent on Rome for electricity. Even if the city's supply was tampered with, unless someone had cut off the power here, or changed the security codes for the locks, her key would access not only this door, but also all those inside.

The benefits of being upper management, she joked inwardly, trying to steady her nerves.

Cautiously, Noemi edged along the warm brick façade. Stories Giulio had shared, on the few occasions he over-imbibed, of his time in Afghanistan, reared up in her head.

Assigned to an American led NATO strike team in Kandahar, he recounted how frequently they had travelled the dusty, narrow, winding roads, through shabby villages, where they were exposed to snipers. A bitter experience, which had prompted him to teach his wife how to recognise when something wasn't right, to be mindful of even the smallest details, and to trust her gut.

While Noemi preferred not to hear about the dangers he had faced, never was she more thankful for his oft-repeated warnings.

Reaching the door, she removed her identification card from around her neck, whispered a small prayer that the key was active, and swiped the electronic pad.

The click of the lock informed her the good Lord, or Fate, or whichever celestial being was in charge of luck was still on her side.

She had no clue her entry had triggered a red light to flick on and off at a recently installed security station, housed in the basement.

Thankful her shoes were soft-soled, Noemi's progress along the tiled halls and up the stairs to her office was soundless. Her keycard granted her access to the labs, but a particular key on her fob was required to open the drug cabinets.

Silent as a ghost, she peered through the glass wall which comprised the corridor side of her office. A frown furrowed her brow.

A tornado would leave less destruction.

Papers were strewn across the floor, and her laptop was not in its usual spot *but*, and importantly to Noemi's assessing gaze, it looked staged, a distraction. The perpetrator was searching for something specific.

Relieved to note her office was empty, she was about to unlock it with the swipe card when she realised someone had beaten her to it with a couple of well-placed shots.

Grimacing, Noemi pushed open the damaged door and hurried to her desk.

While the loss of her laptop was aggravating, it contained nothing of any great importance, they were too easily hacked and a replacement could be procured, if necessary.

A photograph of several people wearing lab coats, herself front and centre, hung askew on the wall. Someone had thought to check behind it for a safe.

Beneath it, her printer stand, which Noemi nudged with her foot. Crouching, she pulled back the carpet, to reveal her floor safe.

Punching in the electronic code, she pressed her thumb against the digital screen, disengaging the secondary lock.

An expensive installation, and one she had felt unwarranted, but her husband convinced her it was worth the cost.

Her coworkers were unaware of its existence, meaning no one would look for it, and, sure enough, her files were in order, including those relating to the detailed and painstaking research pertaining to the virus.

She shoved them into her backpack, then picked up her medical books, which someone had tossed off the shelves.

Is nothing sacred to these arseholes?

The thud of boots thundering up the same stairs she had just ascended, shattered the quiet.

Without pausing to think, she rammed as many books as she could fit into a shopping bag she kept in her desk drawer, and darted out of her office without collecting any of the medical supplies — the reason for her visit in the first place.

Glancing over her shoulder as she ran hell for leather to

the other exit, Noemi spotted a black helmeted figure appearing through the door at the opposite end of the corridor.

"Halt or I'll shoot," a distinctly American voice bellowed.

Noemi ignored it and increased her pace. Reaching the fire-door, she threw herself against it, hearing the sharp rapport of two shots.

Instinctively, she ducked. The first bullet burrowed into the wall in front of her, spraying her with concrete dust.

The second smashed through the small glass window in the door, whizzed past her ear as she jumped over the handrail to... after ricochetting off the solid metallic edge of a step... embed itself in the floor.

Noemi landed on the lower section of the flight of stairs and skidded down a couple of steps, the weight of the back-pack and heavy shopping bag affecting her balance. Scrabbling for the handrail, she managed to avoid an ungainly tumble to the bottom but wrenched her shoulder in the process.

She looked up at the squeal of the fire-door being yanked open, to see the barrel of an automatic weapon above her.

Panting from exertion and fear, she drew the pistol from her jeans, braced herself, against the cold wall, pointed the gun upwards, aimed and, with an unsteady hand, pulled the trigger.

Pain lanced through her shoulder and her shot went wild. Noemi was not trying to hit anyone, she just wanted to delay the shooter long enough to escape.

The shopping bag tucked against her, Noemi emerged onto the ground floor, to be confronted by a group of men running down the corridor.

Unlike Noemi — Fortuna, *aka* Lady Luck, had left the building.

Automatically, she raised the bag like a shield but, by some miracle, the flurry of bullets missed her.

Perhaps the Roman goddess had afforded Noemi the merest smidgen of good fortune before she skedaddled.

It gave Noemi the chance to respond in kind…

…and that's where her luck ran out.

Remembering Giulio's instructions, she fired, hitting the lead gunman in the chest. He dropped to his knees while the others dove for cover, effectively blocking her path to the Staff Room.

Noemi had never shot anything in her life, let alone another human and, now she had, was unsure of her next move.

The voice of her husband bawled in her ear, *"Run."*

Her exit strategy thwarted, Noemi's options were limited. Turning, she flew to the passage which linked the less confidential departments, here at the front of the building to those areas off limits to the public at the rear — but not before she saw her victim get to his feet and ready his weapon.

"A fucking bullet-proof vest," she snarled. "That's just unfair."

In her mad dash, not only did she lose her pursuers in the labyrinth of corridors, but also herself.

Ducking into an alcove to catch her breath, Noemi checked the number on the door opposite. Recognising where she was gave her an idea as to how to effect her escape.

Assured there were no goons approaching, imminently at any rate, she hastened to the next corridor, the far end of which led to the service garage and her only viable way out.

Why such an obvious exit was unguarded did not occur to her… until she reached the door.

Noemi heard the murmur of voices on the other side.

Through the little window set at eye-height, she saw two men in hazmat suits examining the contents of a portable cryofreezer. A piece of *her* equipment, from *her* Level 4 Lab to be exact. It contained assorted vials of pathogens, including Ebola, Marburg virus, Lassa fever, and Bolivian haemorrhagic fever — all of which could kill in a matter of days.

"Why the hell would the boss approve these to be moved, when we already have a damn plague killing everyone indiscriminately? The risk doesn't bear contemplating," Noemi brooded bitterly, adding, "You're not getting paid to ask stupid questions. Just get the hell out of here in one piece."

Engrossed in their discussion, the pair, garbed in PPE, did not hear the click when Noemi swiped her key over the electronic lock, nor noticed her creep behind a stack of cases.

A large, white delivery truck, bearing the logo of a cow smiling inanely and the words *Felice Latteria* circling it, idled in the loading bay, stacked with an abundance of unmarked boxes.

Noemi's brow creased. The portable cryofreezer had its own source of coolant and power, rendering the vehicle's inbuilt refrigeration unit unnecessary. *Why opt for a milk delivery truck?*

Pure obfuscation came the answer. *To conceal what they are actually transporting. Definitely not products from a happy dairy,* Noemi reasoned. *I can't let someone drive away with whatever's in that truck, especially given its camouflage.*

Soundlessly, she skirted the stacks of cases and equipment, hardly daring to breathe until she was at the driver's side door.

In a flash, Noemi was inside. Dropping both bags into the passenger side footwell, she buckled in and slid the gear lever into first. Releasing a weighty exhale, she pressed her foot down hard on the accelerator. The truck lurched forwards, jolting several boxes which tumbled out to scatter across cold concrete of the loading bay, hindering any chance of the shocked personnel giving chase.

Hearing their yells to stop, Noemi was thankful, even if they had guns, that the bulky gloves of their protective gear left them unable to shoot with any accuracy. Relief making her giddy, she stuck her arm out of the open window and flipped them the bird.

The truck careened around the building towards the main exit where Noemi surprised more black-clad men, who scrambled for their weapons, firing haphazardly at the speeding vehicle. Several bullets skimmed the windscreen, the glass quickly resembling a spider's web.

Wrenching the steering wheel to the right, Noemi tried to avoid both men and projectiles realising, too late, she was on course to plough into the SUVs she observed on her arrival.

Wielding a rifle, and with no time to shut the door, one man flung himself into the back seat of the closest vehicle. The heavy truck clipped the door, tearing it from its hinges.

The bumper of the dairy van became lodged in the body shell of the first vehicle, bulldozing it into a second SUV, but the jarring crash released Noemi's truck from the tangle of metal.

With dogged determination, she changed gear and pressed her foot to the floor. As the truck screeched around the curve of the drive, barely missing her VW, she waved goodbye to her past.

Normally, it took about half an hour to drive the eighteen kilometres to Settebagni. Today... not so much. It was worse than the first day of school holidays.

Navigating a road packed with lunatic drivers hellbent on leaving Rome, and liberally littered with abandoned cars, extended that journey by more than two hours.

She had passed homes and businesses destroyed by rioters. "If it is bad now, I fear for our future," she said to the steering wheel.

An empty car park on the outskirts of Settebagni beckoned. It was as good a place as any to check the contents of the truck. Parking under the shade of a stand of trees in one corner, Noemi alighted.

Grasping the handle next to the open rear door, she clambered into the vehicle and inspected several of the cases. They contained narcotics, antibiotics, and, strangely, air-breathing apparatus, complete with extra oxygen canisters.

The assortment of medical supplies, according to the accompanying invoices, were earmarked for the evacuation centre at Taranto.

"Obviously, someone felt they were needed elsewhere." Noemi stopped abruptly, ashamed of being so glib about the theft because those who might have benefitted from this shipment, would not.

In an attempt to ease the pain plaguing her shoulder, which had begun to gnaw at her brain, Noemi considered taking a couple of the Oxycodone she had discovered among the supplies. Common sense reasserted itself and, instead, she opted for two panadeine, found in an adjacent box, nearly choking when she swallowed the pills without water.

Sitting on the bed of the truck, her legs dangling over the edge, she waited for the medication to take effect.

Feeling the discomfort dissipate, marginally, she slid off and secured the doors.

"God knows how much cargo I lost along the way."

Looking to the west, Noemi noticed an ominous cloud bank building.

"Great, on top of everything else, a storm's coming." She scowled. Settling into the cab, she started the engine, then pointed the vehicle in the direction of the resort and her waiting children.

4

Snoring lightly… a trait inherited from their father… Noemi's daughters were tucked up in bed with her. The gentle almost rhythmic sound, cloaked Noemi in a mixture of comfort and grief.

Unable to sleep, the mother of two stared at the ancient cracks in the ceiling. As though the stress of recent events had not already taken its toll on Noemi's psyche, the noisy rattle of the air conditioner's fan rendered a peaceful night's sleep nigh on impossible.

In the darkness, Noemi replayed the events since her arrival at the resort.

The storm had weakened to a soaking rain by the time she reached the castello.

To Noemi's astonishment, the carpark was reasonably full. Either the virus and the resulting civil unrest consuming the surrounding communities had not affected the tourist season, currently at its height, adversely or, and more concerning, the hotel was filled with others of similar intent to hers.

Neither explanation did much to curb her unease.

Relieved to see the space next to Chiara's Fiat was vacant, Noemi manoeuvred the massive truck alongside, and jumped out, landing in a puddle with a splash, soaking her feet and spraying more dirty water to the mud-splattered white panels of the vehicle.

"Crap," she hissed under her breath.

Staring at the execrable weather, Noemi considered making a dash for reception, but something made her hesitate. That anyone outside the lab knew of the theft, was improbable... not something likely to be broadcast... *but, arriving at a holiday resort without the usual paraphanalia might raise eyebrows.*

Flying under the radar was essential.

She mulled over the conundrum, as rain seeped through her jacket... her backpack and the bag of books could not be mistaken for luggage. Then it dawned on her... *the boxes... a couple of those would have to do.*

Climbing into the cargo bay, Noemi wove her way through the jumble of unmarked cases and, without checking the contents, selected a couple which she shoved to the door.

The boxes were heavier than she anticipated but, evidently, Fortuna had decided to play nice again because Noemi came across a hand trolley buried under a pile of overturned cartons.

Lowering the trolley onto the tarmac, she loaded it up.

Now, the real struggle began. The uneven car park caused the trolley, which did not take kindly to the rough surface, to lurch wildly and jerk to a halt with frustrating frequency when loose, wet gravel lodged between wheels and frame, eliciting angry complaints from Noemi about the numbskull who had designed the metal monstrosity.

Thanks in part to the knowledge she was about to see her daughters after such a trying day, she persevered until, blowing a sigh of relief, she entered an airy atrium through a set of sliding glass doors, tracking wet footprints across the polished floor.

Behind the desk sat a solitary figure who looked as haggard as she felt.

"Welcome to Castello di Settebagni," the man greeted in a decidedly disinterested tone. "Do you have a reservation?"

He spotted the stack of rain spattered boxes on the trolley, and not the woman beside it, and continued abrasively, "Look at the mess you're making. Supplies are delivered to the service entrance, and we are not expecting anything today."

Worn out, and irritated by the man's attitude, Noemi retorted, "Noemi Ricci. I am here to join my friends, the Bernardis. I believe they have reserved a room for myself and my daughters."

Wordlessly, the clerk accessed his computer. "Oh. Here it is. It's lucky they saw fit to book you a room. We are, as usual, inundated at this time of the season," his tone a trifle oily. "Your friends opted for a non-smoking floor. That ok?"

"Perfectly."

He slid a keycard across the counter with the instructions. "Room 312. The Bernardis are across the hall in 315."

She picked up the plastic rectangle, then paused.

Registering the newcomer seemed frozen in place, the clerk asked wearily, "Is there something else you need?"

"Assistance with my luggage would be nice," Noemi sniped.

The man shrugged. "The porter failed to come in this morning, and we have no extra staff available. Regrettably, you will have to attend to your own belongings." Sounding anything but contrite. "The elevator is down the hall, to your left."

Inwardly, Noemi threatened, *Just wait until you read the scathing review I intend to leave on the net about this place.* Not stopping to contemplate the likelihood of anyone actually reading it… or, indeed, whether there would be a functioning internet when she tried to submit it.

The cart in her room, boxes stored out of sight, and the room locked, Noemi knocked on the door numbered 315.

A bedraggled Chiara answered at the first rap. Her face, reminiscent of a clown, no doubt courtesy of Bianca, caused Noemi to convulse with mirth. At this point, a welcome emotion.

Chiara's brow knitted into an angry arch. "I'm glad you find this funny. If you dare leave me in charge of your children again, I shall sell them to Santino's people as circus freaks."

Ignoring Chiara's idle threat, Noemi's gaze slid over her friend's shoulder to see her similarly painted toddler.

Recognising the laughter, Bianca bolted across the carpet, carolling, "Mama, Mama, look what Auntie Carey and me were doing." Hugging her mother around the knees, the child smeared makeup all over Noemi's jeans.

The sound of her mother's voice had the opposite effect on Sophia who burst into fractious sobs; a clear indication her voracious appetite required staunching. Lifting the youngest Ricci into her arms and nestling her close, Noemi's lips curved in a fleeting smile at the domesticity of the scene.

She suggested to Chiara, "Why don't you clean yourself

up and meet us in the bistro downstairs in about half an hour."

Bianca clinging to her leg like a limpet, Noemi returned to her room, little girl's giggles echoing along the empty corridor.

The hand scrawled note taped to the bistro's door read: *No Kitchen Staff - Self Serve.*

Noemi checked the reception desk. The clerk from earlier was nowhere to be seen.

No help there then.

Carrying Sophia, Noemi ushered her older daughter into the salon, spotting at least a dozen fellow diners eating some sort of sandwich, bottled water at their elbows.

The discrepancy between the number of diners and the number of vehicles in the car park, prompted Noemi to wonder whether there was a restaurant close by. That said, herding her children through the rain did not appeal.

Suppressing the almost overwhelming desire for a plateful of cacio e pepe, the cheese and pepper pasta dish, which was a staple in the Ricci household, Noemi was about to ask those at the nearest table where they had found the food, when Bianca called her over to an ornately carved wooden sideboard.

Piled on platters, mounds of pathetic-looking sand-wiches. Bianca reached up on her tiptoes and plucked one from the closest tray.

She peeled apart the sliced ciabatta, scrunching up her nose in distaste. "Eww, bendy cheese. Not even any porscutto. Mama, let's go someplace else… this looks yucky."

"Hush, now, poppet. Just eat it tonight and we'll find something better tomorrow."

The answer did not sit well with Bianca, who grimaced, preparing to protest in the inimitable way characteristic of two-year-olds when thwarted and surrounded by strangers, even if she was four. This only meant she possessed two extra years of practice.

Noemi cut Bianca off before she could start, warning, "Don't you dare think about it. Otherwise, no swimming with Aunty Chiara."

A voice behind Noemi interjected, "Did I hear my name used in vain?"

In a doleful wail, the little girl pled her case, in as adult a manner as she could muster, "Mama is making me eat these 'gusting sammiches. They're stinky and I fink p'robly howwid."

Nicoletta perched on her hip, Chiara offered her free hand to Bianca. "I wouldn't eat those either. Let's leave your meanie mama here and see what's in the kitchen."

Before Noemi could object, the trio disappeared through the swinging metal door at the end of the room.

They returned minutes later, a gleeful Bianca toting a box of assorted gelato in wafer cups.

"Look, Mama... we got yummy stuff. I even got some for Sophia."

Noemi narrowed her eyes. "Thanks for turning my daughter into a thief."

Chiara shot her an innocent smile. "Consider it more teaching her to scavenge for necessities."

Using one of Chiara's favourite Americanisms against her, Noemi huffed and flapped a hand at her friend with a long-suffering, "Whatever."

They settled at one of the tables by the exit to the pool,

where Santino joined them, munching one of the questionable sandwiches and carrying a stack of others.

Her mouth full of gelato, Bianca mumbled an incomprehensible warning about the food, but no one paid any attention. Aggrieved, she sat back and waited for her adopted uncle to turn purple and throw up, astonished when he finished his first sandwich and began to eat another.

By the time he had consumed his third, Bianca's stomach was rumbling… the gelato not as filling as she expected.

Softly, she asked, "Uncle Santi, may I have a sammich, too?"

Chuckling, Santino handed her one, reassuring, "They taste better than they look, poppet."

Relieved Santino had persuaded Bianca to partake of the meagre spread. After Noemi and Chiara had settled the other two infants, the three adults discussed the plans for the near future.

Several people came through the door from the indoor pool, some of whom had racking coughs, most not making any effort to cover their mouths with their hands.

Glaring daggers, the three adults fell silent and shifted in their seats to form a protective screen around their children, until the newcomers moved on to sit at tables nearer the food, effectively curbing any thoughts of additional helpings.

Giving the guests the evil eye, Chiara growled under her breath, "Remind me not to let kids touch anything." Following up with a meditative, "Once I have decontaminated this place thoroughly…"

Not only Noemi's research assistant, Chiara Bernardi was also head of Ringtonwoth Pharmaceuticals Emergency Response Team. While she often joked that this role had taught her to eliminate her enemies without leaving a trace, when a crisis arose, and there had been a few, she was first on scene, managing her crew with dictatorial efficiency. A good ally in an emergency.

"...I think we should stay put for the time being. There's plenty of food in the kitchen—"

Santino, who had contributed little to the conversation so far, disagreed delicately, "No, dragul meu…" slipping into his ancestral gypsy tongue as he addressed the love of his life. "…we may be safe for now but, if others become aware food is stored here, I doubt this place can withstand a raid."

An appraisal attested to by the guests who seemed intent on devouring their quota and then some, leaving scarcely a handful of sandwiches on the tray.

"See what I mean?" Santino tutted disapprovingly. "We cannot expect anyone to share supplies — at least, not here. We'd do better trying to reach Florence or perhaps Genoa. The local carabinieri will protect us, and it's got to be safer than trying to survive on our own. I bet they've already set up a food distribution plan."

"Like they did in Rome?" Chiara snorted sarcastically.

"There were too many people and not enough services," he countered. "Those cities are less populated."

"Maybe," Noemi conceded, "but not by much."

"Still less than Rome," he reiterated.

Reluctantly, both women conceded his point, although Noemi added a proviso, "If there's no staff by the morning, we take whatever non-perishables we can get our hands on and, if the rain has stopped, leave as quickly as possible."

"By the looks of the pantry, they're pretty well-stocked," Chiara said.

"Yet you gave Bianca gelato," Noemi reminded scathingly.

Santino ignored their banter. "We have a plan, then? Also, I recommend turning in now, so we can get an early start."

Bianca denounced that suggestion. "Bed? Mama promised I could go swimmin' with Aunty."

Santino tried to explain, "The pool is not good to swim in, micuțul—"

"Do not *little one* me," the little girl retorted, bringing the conversation to a halt.

"Bianca Ricci. First, apologise for being rude, and second, how do you know what that word means?" Noemi asked.

"She must have heard it before," Chiara chimed in.

"Nuh uh." Bianca beamed. "My brain told me."

No one at the table understood that this was merely a foreshadowing of what the future had in store for them.

For now, they wrote it off, presuming the girl had learnt the phrase from one of the adults.

5

Noemi bolted upright. Something had disturbed her. She shook her head, amazed, given their circumstances, she had drifted off sometime during the night.

The pitiful wheeze of one of her daughter's fighting to breathe, accompanied by a hoarse cough banished the last dregs of sleep.

Noemi switched on the bedside lamp and leant over the little girl. Her chest pinched in terror at the sight of Bianca's blue-tinged lips.

Instinctively, she checked Sophia. The infant lay motionless, her lips the same hue as her sister's.

Draping Bianca over her arm, Noemi slammed the heel of her palm against her daughter's back. Frothy fluid spewed out of the child's mouth, staining the duvet. Her breathing seemed to slow to a raspy rattle.

Noemi turned to Sophia. Not feeling a pulse, she performed CPR on her baby. Reciting every prayer she had learnt in Catholic school between breaths, especially that she could avoid breaking her daughter's tiny ribs, Sophia's guttural gasp for air, followed by her banshee scream flooded Noemi with relief… but it was temporary.

Frowning, she tried to isolate the cause of her children's malaise. Replaying the days' events, she pinned the blame solely on the coughing guests from the dining room.

She threatened malevolently, "If I see you again, it won't be whatever illness you contracted which takes your life."

Refocusing on her daughters, she forced her panicked mother's brain to surrender to her calm, astute, scientific brain.

Examining both girls more thoroughly, she took note of the symptoms:

Temperature… elevated.

Skin… clammy, but no rash.

Breathing… with difficulty.

Cough… croupy.

Lips… still blue, but less so.

Throat… swollen and red.

Eyes… cloudy, unfocused.

Noemi's heart sank. She was all too familiar with this mysterious ailment; she had seen it claim the lives of her lab rats time and again.

There was no mistaking it. The insidious virus, which the authorities believed relatively contained, had invaded with a greater aggression than any hostile power could hope to wield.

What puzzled Noemi was the incubation period was all wrong for the girls to have contracted it here. Typically, and similar to the common cold or influenza, the virus manifested three to four days after coming into contact with an infected individual, and the victim remained contagious for several subsequent days.

The number of people who could be afflicted in a small window of time was astronomical.

She had taken a week's holiday to spend time with the girls, but the abysmal weather had kept them indoors for the duration, they had not even ventured out to the supermarket. Their only visitors, her friends who had popped in the night Giulio died.

The only person who had mixed with others on a daily basis was Giulio.

Was he the carrier?

"But how? He showed none of the classical symptoms. Is it possible for someone to be asymptomatic with this virus… let alone a carrier?" she muttered, second-guessing herself.

Questions she could not answer.

Knowing the girls' time was limited, and feeling less than stellar, Noemi rummaged through the cardboard boxes hoping to find something, anything to clear the children's airways.

Opening the first box, she was astounded to discover it brim full of Ringtonwoth Pharmaceuticals' variation of the vaccine. Hundreds of single doses, sealed in foil, and marked for delivery to the evacuation centre in the south.

Thunderstruck, she rocked back on her heels. "Oh my God. How did the company manage this without anybody noticing?"

While this find might be helpful in the future, at this point it was too late. Noemi continued to dig through the boxes.

In the third one, she unearthed the breathing equipment she had seen in the back of the truck, unaware whether she had purloined masks suitable for both children and adults.

Her luck held.

In amongst the adult masks, she found those for children, most nestled inside the larger ones, along with spare canisters.

Noemi pulled out three in sizes to suit. Despite her

tongue swelling, blocking her airway, she flouted the instructions given by every airline attendant ever, and positioned one on each of the girl's faces, then activated them, *before* putting on her own.

Her vision was beginning to dim, as her oxygen deprived brain struggled to keep her conscious.

Finally, she cinched her mask in place.

The cool blast of pure oxygen, released from the small, attached canister, filled her nostrils and mouth. As it passed over her tongue, she felt her windpipe widen, her breathing became less laboured and returned to normal... curiously, a response contrary to her research. Supplying oxygen to the experimental rats only appeared to hasten their voyage across the Styx. At that moment, she did not give a flying fu... damn about the why's and wherefores... she could breathe.

As her vision cleared and her mind sharpened, Noemi's ears caught peculiar sounds penetrating the thin walls of the hotel, echoing Bianca's strangled croaks.

She pondered the gestation of the virus, ticking off the sequence of progression in her head, at the same time as her maternal instinct interrupted, screaming, *Now is not the time. Check on your friends, then get the hell out of here.*

Scooping her ailing daughters off the bed, and grabbing a handful of masks, Noemi dashed into the corridor.

Refusing to set her children on the floor, Noemi kicked the door of 315, nearly breaking the flimsy veneer panel.

Santino opened the door. Half-asleep, his hair was a mass of damp, dark curls, framing his face, which had a waxy pallor. The sclera of his brown eyes was already bloodshot, and his breathing strained.

Before he could demand an explanation, Noemi smacked a mask against his stomach. "Don't waste air asking, just put it on."

Brushing past him without another word, she examined Chiara and Nicoletta. It was one thing for her friend to be exposed to the virus at work, but that she might have contracted it when attempting to help save Giulio's life, weighed heavily on Noemi's heart.

Noemi set Bianca in a chair, and handed Sophia to the now masked Santino, who had joined her next to the bed.

Kneeling beside Nicoletta, Noemi registered the baby's hoarse whimpers intermingled with a fluid-filled cough. At least she was breathing, albeit a struggle, a glance at the Chiara told Noemi she was unresponsive.

Aware children had no reserve when it came to severe infections, and deterioration was far more rapid than in adults, Noemi turned Nicoletta onto her side and worked to clear the infant's airway of the same frothy fluid she had dislodged from Bianca's throat.

Once the toddler inhaled without restriction, Noemi secured a mask on her. The muffled cries grew stronger as the oxygen forced its way into Nicoletta's lungs.

Handing the baby to Santino, who was trying to juggle two squirming children, she said, "Do not dare lay either of them down yet. I need to make sure their airways stay clear."

Now it was Chiara's turn.

Feeling for a pulse, Noemi found it thready and rapid, giving up trying to keep count when it exceeded 120 beats per minute.

Her exclamation slipped out before she could help herself, "Fuck, tachycardia."

"What?" Santino demanded, wanting verification of what he thought he had heard.

"Tachycardia. The virus is pounding Chiara's heart to death."

Her research indicated the immediate commencement of CPR in an attempt to slow a sufferer's heart to a survivable rate. Regrettably, Noemi soon realised she needed to take more drastic measures.

"Santino, get your ass down to the front desk and check for an automated external defibrillator."

To which, Santino shot his friend a *what the hell am I supposed to do with these two* look.

With a huff, Noemi relieved him of the two crying bundles and settled them with Bianca. The four-year-old's big sister mode kicked in, and she rocked the pair to a respectable silence, allowing Noemi to resume her resuscitation and Santino to head downstairs.

When Santino returned with the AED, he found his wife on the floor, her blouse ripped open, and Noemi performing CPR vigorously. Kneeling on the carpet across from Noemi, he prepped the unit. As a soldier, he was trained to operate these if required.

While Noemi paused chest compressions long enough to give Chiara two quick breaths, Santino placed the AED's pads on his wife. One on the upper right side and the other on the lower left, then activated the *Charge* button.

When Noemi finished the next cycle of CPR, Santino ordered, "Clear."

Both sat back as he pressed the discharge button. The high-pitched whine culminated in a loud *thunk* and Chiara's body bowed upwards momentarily. The life-saving machine measured her heart rhythm and advised to continue with CPR.

Charging the unit, Santino repeated the process, sending another surge of electrical energy through his wife's body. This time Chiara's heart reverted to a stable rhythm.

Although her pulse grew stronger with each beat, Chiara did not regain consciousness. Noemi fixed a mask over her friend's face, hoping the oxygen would revive her.

The instant she was confident Chiara was breathing on her own, Noemi, winded and lightheaded from the exertion, replaced her own mask.

As exhaustion and anxiety staked their claims, neither Noemi nor Santino could be sure whether Chiara had suffered any irreversible effects owing to the length of time she was without oxygen.

All they could was pray… which was all anyone could do regarding the fate of the Italian Peninsula.

It was a long night. Noemi replaced the oxygen cartridges on all the masks, monitoring everyone until confident they were no longer needed, but worry that any one of them might deteriorate made for a restless night.

Shortly before the inky blue darkness yielded to the pearlescent hues of dawn, she succumbed to fatigue and slept.

The soft light heralding the sunrise danced behind Noemi's eyelids. Childishly, she squeezed them closed. If she did not open them, she could pretend the last forty-eight hours was nothing more than a bad dream.

A solid foot to her ankle, along with an aggrieved, "Ouch, dammit," jolted her awake.

Peeling her eyes open, Noemi saw the slender frame of Chiara towering over her.

"Care to explain why I went to sleep in a comfortable bed

but ended up on the floor, feeling like I'd been run over by a bus and kicked by a bull?" Chiara demanded.

"Good morning to you too," Noemi grumbled. Sitting up, she stretched, her aching muscles protesting. "Ooof. A *thank you* for saving *your* life would be appreciated."

With no memory of the previous night's excitement, Chiara gawked in disbelief.

"Just take it easy, you may well have cracked ribs," Noemi cautioned, aware she had to apprise her friend of the details,.

"Because… and that might explain the bruising." Chiara frowned, rubbing the tender skin on her chest gingerly.

"How about we check out the kitchen and see whether they have any orange juice or coffee left, while I bring you up to speed on your brush with death. Here," Noemi gave Chiara a mask, "might be an idea to wear one of these."

6

———

Her voice slightly distorted by the mask, Noemi explained the previous night's drama to her best friend as they wound their way along the maze of corridors, noting as they walked that the resort was oddly devoid of other guests and staff.

Entering the quiet kitchen, the scattered mess spoke of others having the same idea.

Cupboard doors hung open. The pantry door stood ajar. Anything not edible was discarded on the floor. Along with the rejected supplies, smears of blood here and there suggested people had tussled over what was available.

Fortunately, the room was empty, allowing the two women to conduct a thorough search before anyone else appeared.

While the erstwhile scavengers had raided the coolers, liberating them of meats, and sundry dairy products...all of which would go bad in a short time...it appeared those foods which might take a modicum of effort to prepare had been ignored.

Taking a cursory glance into the pantry, Noemi spotted

another door. Expecting it to be an exit, she was pleasantly surprised when it opened into a storage room. "Chiara, would you get a load of this," she called to her friend.

They stood, shoulder to shoulder, sighing in admiration at the sight. In front of them, stacked neatly on the shelves, boxes of canned tomatoes, soup, and tins of fruit, along with sacks of rice and pasta.

"Well, praise all the Gods," A smile lit Chiara's pinched features. "Best not forget the can openers."

Relief at finding this stash led to their next quest for sustenance.

Desperate for a decent coffee to ease her fraught nerves, Noemi spotted an industrial-size machine, miraculously intact, plenty of beans in the dispenser. Topping up the water, she listened to the glorious burble and breathed in the heavenly aroma of brewing coffee, while she foraged around the kitchen.

Pulling a large butcher's knife from its block, Noemi studied the sharpened blade for a moment.

Her husband used to joke, as he diced vegetables in their kitchen, "You never know when you might need a good knife." Never had a seemingly random statement rung so true.

A soft hiss from the coffee maker brought her back to the moment. Filling two mugs, she handed one to Chiara who quirked an incredulous brow.

Reasonably certain the virus was not loitering in the kitchen waiting to pounce, Noemi removed her mask and swallowed a large mouthful of the devil's brew, as she referred to it. The caffeine fired along her synapses, working its magic.

Chiara's eyes widened.

"What?" Noemi shrugged and indicated the cartridge. "The oxygen is low, and we cannot rely on these masks for ever. Look around us, it's not as though we're in a cloud of toxins… at least I don't think so. Ok, so to date, we haven't identified all the modes of transmission, but are we going to wash our hands? Absolutely. Are we going to lick the surfaces? Not on your Nelly. We just need to be careful.

"Plus, I need coffee," she infused a convincing note into her voice.

That Noemi did not drop dead in front of her, persuaded Chiara to follow suit, gulping a lungful of the fresh air wafting in, and savouring the aroma of the fresh brew. Her senses snapped into life. "Oh, that's better. I hate the feel of these things." She glared at the offending article.

"It did save your life," Noemi reminded, tartly.

Refreshed by her first two cups, Noemi sent Chiara up to the room, complete with a packet of biscuits, uncovered in a corner of the pantry, far enough back to be missed in a less exhaustive search.

Might not be the healthiest breakfast fare but will suffice until we can find something more substantial, Noemi justified internally.

As luck would have it, while appropriating several saucepans and a kettle, Chiara had come across a stack of brand-new thermos flasks, still in their boxes. Crowing with glee, she unpacked them and rinsed them thoroughly with boiling water.

"We're going to need more coffee," she trilled, waving one at Noemi, hitting the pans piled on the bench top, causing an ear-aching clang. "Oops." She blushed.

"I think you've had enough," Noemi teased. Taking the

offending article before Ciara demolished the kitchen, she stood it under the nozzle of the machine.

The thermos filled with the dark-roasted gold, she screwed on the lid and handed it to Chiara. "Take this to your dearly beloved. Ought to be enough caffeine in there to get him moving. Without exacerbating the damage to your ribs, can you figure out what to feed the kids?"

"Leave it with me." Chiara grinned, "What are you gonna do?"

"Bring the truck around to that door." Noemi pointed to the rear exit. "That way we don't have to carry all this shit through the hotel. If we can't fit everything in, there's your car."

"I like your thinking." Chiara nodded and was gone, the door swinging shut behind her.

Her departure left the kitchen eerily quiet.

Noemi shivered. "We need to get out of here," she muttered ominously.

Tucking a second thermos of coffee under her arm, Noemi tracked through the hotel to the main entrance.

Rain pounded against the glass façade. "A break in the weather might be nice," she sniped at the heavens.

Dreading the thought of getting soaked again, she searched behind the empty reception desk for an umbrella or a poncho, finding one stashed in a small cubby. Shaking it out, Noemi pulled the wrinkly red vinyl over her head and headed for the car park.

There were fewer cars than the previous night; some guests had left. Fleetingly, she hoped they were doing okay, beset with the uneasy feeling several more would never check out.

Dashing to the truck, Noemi paused at the rear of the vehicle, wondering whether she ought to organise it now or wait until she was at the service doors.

Aware it would take a few minutes for Santino to get to the kitchen, she seized the opportunity to tidy up the interior.

It took longer than she expected, and her joints ached with the effort of shifting heavy boxes. Noemi could not decide whether this was related to the virus, or the damp air. Unable to answer her own question, she ignored it and concentrated on the task at hand.

Satisfied she had created enough space, she secured the door, climbed into the driver's seat, and tossed the thermos across to the passenger side.

Starting the engine, she circled the hotel, coming to a halt at the delivery entrance.

Grateful for the broad porch, Noemi reversed carefully, spotting, in her side mirror, a veritable tower of boxes which looked to be almost twice her height. Unbidden, she was reminded of the game *Jenga*, prompting her to smother a chuckle at the image of herself trying to slide out one of the lower boxes without the whole thing collapsing.

Jumping out, she rounded the truck, cursing whoever's bright idea it was to pile the damn boxes so high, to swallow a startled squawk when Bianca popped out from behind it, munching a biscuit. The little girl clicked her heels together, stood at something resembling attention, and threw her mother a smart salute.

Flabbergasted, Noemi quizzed, without frightening her daughter, "Poppet, why are you here by yourself?"

Gleefully, the girl declared, "I'm not by myself, Uncle Santi made me a soldier like him and Papa. He told me to hide here..." indicating a spot behind the stack, "...and to fetch him quick sharp if I saw anyone 'cept you.

"Said I was a sentry or something like that. Anyway, he told me I was..." she crinkled her nose in concentration, "...smart enough to be a gen'ral. That means I'm more 'portant than papa *and* uncle, and I just started."

Noemi chuckled at Bianca's exuberant expression. "And where, by chance, is your aunty?"

"Oh, she's with the babies. *This* is grownup stuff, and they are too small." Bianca puffed out her chest.

"I am impressed. You are certainly qualified for your new rank. How about asking your uncle to help load the truck?"

Saluting once more, Bianca skipped into the kitchen, shouting, "Uncle Santi, come out, come out wherever you are."

Shaking her head tolerantly, she watched her daughter disappear into the back of the resort, then studied the imposing stack. At first, she contemplated shoving it over, taking the chance the contents would escape relatively unscathed.

"No harm in a dented can or two," Noemi reasoned, preparing to reduce the fortification to rubble.

Her hand was on the middle box when a blood-curdling shriek rang out from the kitchen.

Noemi spun about to see a dishevelled man brandishing a knife, and obviously in the grip of the virus, forcing Bianca through the door.

Through coughing fits, the man yelled at Noemi, "You there, if you d-don't want me to hurt this little girl, do as I say."

Appalled, Noemi controlled her shock to appeal, "Please, please, let her go. She's suffered enough."

The man grabbed Bianca by the shoulder and held her against him, commanding, "In that case do not argue with me. Get your ass in that truck, and the three of us will take a nice ride, somewhere safe."

"Sir, let her go, and I will take you wherever you want. Just don't hurt her."

"Sh-shut up and move it. I will not tell you again."

Noemi was frozen in place. Not only out of fear but also, and overriding her terror, anger that this man was using a child… *her child*… as a human shield.

Weighing the odds that, in his present condition, she could take him on and save Bianca, the world came to a standstill when the click of a pistol's hammer being engaged interrupted the tableau.

The barrel of Santino's *Beretta 92FS* pistol was pressed to the man's right temple. Neither Noemi nor the would-be hijacker had noticed him appear from the kitchen.

"Sir," the word was devoid of emotion, "if *you* wish to escape in one piece, let my niece go."

"L-like h-hell I will," the man spat. "St-step back and d-drop your gun b-before I slice up this little girl."

"I am afraid the child's mother will not forgive me if I do."

"Th-then her blood is on—"

The report from the pistol curtailed the man's last words as the bullet penetrated his temple and erupted out of the opposite side of his skull.

Bianca gave vent to an hysterical scream as her kidnapper relaxed his grip and crumpled to the ground behind her. Noemi rushed forwards to sweep her daughter into her arms.

While she attempted to calm the child, Santino kept his pistol at the ready in case the thief had not come alone.

Satisfied the coast was clear, he instructed, "Fetch Chiara and the babies. We need to leave."

By the time Noemi reached Chiara's room, Bianca was a sobbing mess. She retreated into her shell, refusing to speak to her mother.

Noemi could not fathom whether the four-year-old was capable of processing what had just happened. It was one thing to contend with the death of her papa, but to witness the taking of a life… even though Santino's quick reaction had saved hers… quite another.

Unsure what to do, Noemi settled Bianca into one of the chairs, registering the glassy look in Bianca's normally mischievous gaze.

She explained the disturbing incident to Chiara who managed to quash the litany of questions threatening to spill over her lips, making do with, "Ok, I need details, but not right now. Feed Sophia, then I'll stay here with the kids while you get your belongings from the other room."

Torn between tending to her daughter's trauma, and fleeing this hotel, Noemi knew the latter was of greater imperative and nodded her agreement.

Wheeling the loaded hand-trolley to the kitchen, Noemi left the transfer of boxes in Santino's capable hands and returned to the room to help Chiara with the small-fry, and the rest of their luggage.

The boot of Chiara's car was full almost to the roof, leaving Noemi concerned it was blocking their line of sight through the rear-view mirror. A concern not alleviated when Chiara ground the gears into reverse, making the car jerk.

Biting her lip, Noemi kept her counsel but leapt out of the car with alacrity when Chiara drew up at the rear of the building.

She did not care what Santino had secured in the truck, she just wanted to get the hell out of here.

Santino called, "Are you sure you don't want to ride with Chiara? I can take the truck."

Noemi shook her head and clambered into the driver's seat. Starting the engine, she rolled her window down long enough to say, "I need you to drive your car. I cannot trust Chiara to keep the car on the road in this weather."

"Where are we headed?" Santino, aware of his wife's lead foot, inquired.

"As agreed, we'll aim for Florence. From there, who knows."

7

Word of the government's abdication spread through the Italian peninsula like a wildfire, leaving an indelible scar across the landscape. As the group travelled north towards Florence, they witnessed, first hand, the devastation the collapse of a civilisation wrought.

In the blink of an eye, towns were ravaged. Smoke billowed from the broken windows of businesses which had been looted and set ablaze. Scavengers picked through abandoned vehicles, like vultures, in a desperate attempt to find sustenance, however meagre.

Everywhere, militia appeared. While most appeared to be farmers and townsfolk more interested in scaring strangers away from their homes and businesses, it was not true of everyone.

Outside Orvieto, they encountered three soldiers sitting aboard a PUMA, armed with *ARX160* automatic rifles and a mounted .50 calibre machine gun. The vehicle was angled perpendicular to the road, forcing the mini convoy to come to a stop.

A man sporting *maggiore* stripes, jumped down from the PUMA, readying his weapon as he approached Santino's car.

Noemi held her breath.

The man scarcely gave the Fiat a glance, directing Santino to, "Stay put," when he saw the driver's door pop open as he passed.

Instead of questioning the woman driving the truck, the guard disappeared around the rear.

Noemi watched the door swing back to clang against the side panel, and presumed he was checking the contents. Her nerves already strained, stretched taut like an overwound clock.

She saw him poke his head around the side, and their eyes met through the wing-mirror. He approached her window and tapped it with his rifle barrel.

"Eh, bella signora, it appears you have climbed into the wrong vehicle…"

Hearing the the soldier tell Noemi to get out, Santino shifted in his seat, his senses on high alert as he was faced with a grim choice. Either shoot the man beside Noemi's window and risk being slaughtered by the mounted machine gun or kill the two on the vehicle and sacrifice Noemi.

He signalled for his wife to slide his pistol over without making it apparent to the pair on the PUMA.

He was unaware Noemi had chosen a third option.

"…so, if you will join me out here and bring the keys."

Noemi refused to move.

The soldier cocked his rifle and rapped the glass harder. "I said, get out." He grasped the door handle and yanked it open.

The blast from Giulio's *Beretta* lit the man's face as the bullet tore through his brain.

No one had noticed Noemi withdraw the pistol from her waistband to press the barrel against the door. She knew, given the distance between the soldier and herself, accuracy was not essential, hitting him anywhere above the shoulders would suffice.

As the 9MM exploded by the truck's door, Santino leapt from his car to dispatch the other two soldiers.

He heard the report of a gun behind him ring out again. Instinctively ducking, Santino spun about, pistol aimed in defence. Presuming the soldier had survived somehow and was shooting Noemi, he was shocked to see the latter standing on the truck's running board, firing bullets into the major's corpse.

Hurrying over, he stopped Noemi before she could empty the clip, and pried the weapon from her grip.

Unable to kill the soldier any further, she slumped onto the seat. The sound of the girls' wailing, caused by the din of the shootout, floated to her from the Bernardis' car. Tears threatened and, as the stark reality of their situation hit home, she stopped trying to be strong and gave into a bout of weeping.

Santino left her to cry it out, and went to help Chiara soothe the children.

He wanted to tell Noemi that first kills are always the hardest but surmised she had just learned that lesson.

Sliding out of the truck, Noemi gave the bloodied body an abhorrent glare. Had Santino not taken the clip of the pistol before he handed it back to her, she would have shot the soldier once more for good measure.

Instead, she kicked the dead man, muttering, "I hope you rot in hell, you bastard."

When she reached the car, Bianca and Nicoletta, aside from an occasional hiccup, had calmed down, while Sophia, as was her habit, remained blissfully unaware, sleeping the sleep of the innocent.

In an attempt to distract, she mustered up a cheerful

smile and said, in as convincing a manner as possible, "Goodness me they were loud fireworks."

The two girls, who had not witnessed the actual shooting, stared at her wide-eyed, and Nicoletta, with typical insouciance, quizzed, "Is it a party, Aunty Neemi?"

"Something like that," Chiara interposed with a dramatic eye roll.

"Ohhhhh, can we watch them?" Bianca jiffled on her seat in excitement; she hated missing out.

"Maybe another day," Noemi placated. "We still have a long way to go."

Leaning on the back of the Fiat, Santino asked, a trifle sarcastically, "You still think it's safer to head north?"

"Yes, even more so now, but I think we should get off the A1 and take the SR2 instead. I doubt many people will take that route."

"Will you let me drive the truck?" he pressed. "You go with Chiara."

This earned him an elbow in the ribs from his wife, which did not go unnoticed by Noemi. Surmising, correctly as it happened, that Chiara would trust a raging bull to drive the car over Noemi in her current state, the latter grinned. "No, I'm good to drive, except I'm taking the lead, in case we run across any more of these impromptu blockades."

As they prepared to backtrack to the pertinent junction, Chiara studied the PUMA speculatively. "It's a shame to leave that shiny toy sitting there."

"Somebody will collect it soon enough, sweetheart," Santino reassured.

"I suppose, but why should it not be us? That gun looks like it could come in handy."

"It didn't do those three any good, did it?" Santino pointed out. "Never mind that they are petrol guzzlers, how are we supposed to strap the girls in?"

"Well, what about mounting that peashooter on top of our car?"

Santino shook his head in disbelief at his wife's suggestion but did bring the car to a halt, honking at Noemi to do the same.

Alighting, he clambered up the PUMA and disappeared inside.

Chiara's perplexed tones reached him through the open turret. "Santino Bernardi, it was a joke. Get your ass out of there this minute."

Rooting through the inner compartment of the PUMA, he heard Noemi ask his wife, "What the hell is he doing? Does he think we actually need one of those monstrosities?"

"I was kidding," Chiara replied, explaining, "What I really wanted was that awesome cap gun up there." She pointed to the .50 calibre machine gun.

"Found something more useful," Santino's voice echoed from the depths of the tank.

Reappearing, he hoisted up a dark green case and set it on the vehicle, "Ammo for the rifles. I also found a couple of clips for the pistols and some *Ka-Bar* knives.

"Looks like our friends here were not genuine soldiers, at least not members of the Italian armed forces."

"Mercenaries?" Noemi quizzed, not entirely surprised at how quickly *civilian contractors* had *offered their resources…* whether required or not. "Why do you say that?"

"The knives are American," Chiara answered for her husband.

Noemi opened her mouth to ask how she knew, but Chiara anticipated the question.

"I just do." She had no intention of revealing how, during his military training, her brother was killed by a fellow recruit wielding a Ka-Bar knife in a drunken rage; something Santino already knew about.

Loading the weapons and ammunition into the truck's bed, he got back in his car. "If we could, ladies. The day's a-wasting."

The group turned north on the SR2, a route which proved no less fraught.

Entering Siena, Noemi was forced to accelerate to ram the truck through a roadblock manned by armed militia. The impact buckled the front edge of the bonnet, which crumpled inwards against the radiator.

Bullets ricocheted and buzzed through the panelling, popping cans of food and leaving the smiling cow with missing teeth, a pierced ear, and a hole between its eyes. One projectile punctured the condenser, releasing refrigerant gas from the hole in a loud hiss.

Tempted to return fire, Noemi was smart enough to acknowledge the situation did not allow for a foolhardy gunfight. The best she could do was speed through the city.

The Bernardis fared little better. Glass shards peppered the interior of their Fiat. Unbuckling her belt, Chiara spun in her seat and, ignoring the agony lancing through her bruised chest, leant over to release the girls from their car seats, pushing them to the floor.

She exhorted Bianca to, "Make sure you and the babies stay low." then shrieked, "Ahhhhhhhhh," when a bullet pierced the metal of the door, barely missing her femoral artery as it buried itself in her thigh. "Really, weren't my broken ribs enough," she bellowed as, frantically, she scrabbled for something to act as a tourniquet.

Santino shoved Chiara, who was swearing like a trooper, into the passenger-side footwell. Noemi might not have the skill to shoot while driving like a bat out of hell, the same was not true for him.

His family under imminent threat, Santino rolled down his window and returned fire. At the speeds they were travelling, Santino was keenly aware hitting anything would be nigh on impossible, but pinning the bastards down would suffice.

One glance at Chiara informed him his wife was trying to stem the blood flow with her top, and another in the mirror told him Bianca was doing her best to keep the other girls safe. That they had placed so much responsibility on a four-year-old, broke his heart, but they had no choice.

He prayed the stress would not cause his niece undue trauma.

Making it to the northern side of Siena, Noemi smashed through the barricade in no less violent a fashion, the unsuspecting guards bolting in all directions, with Santino right behind her. The smaller car bounced over the debris wildly, but they had made it.

Seconds later they were clear of the city and speeding away in the late afternoon light.

Not far from Florence, Noemi noticed a red light flashing on her dashboard. Squinting, she saw her temperature gauge was well past *H*, and white steam billowed from the radiator.

She slapped the steering wheel in frustration. No doubt, as well as being damaged when she ran the blockades, someone had got off a lucky shot.

"Arseholes!"

8

___

Noemi nursed the dying, pseudo-milk truck to the nearest service station. In its final death throes, the beast limped onto a forecourt cluttered with vehicles. Signs declaring *No Petrol* clung to some of the pumps.

Chaos reigned. Nozzles ripped from their hoses, presumably as a result of frustrated patrons driving off in angry haste, lay in twisted heaps on the concrete. Vehicles, undoubtedly abandoned after their owners were unable to squeeze even a drop of fuel from the bowsers, created an impromptu maze.

In spite of everything, Noemi felt her lips twitch. The scene looked like a fractious child had thrown their toys in the air and stamped their foot in utter pique, upon hearing the service station had the audacity to run out of petrol.

Noemi was as thankful for the mayhem as she was for reaching the service station. It made hiding the truck in plain sight easier.

She coaxed the ailing vehicle into a parking spot park just

as it sputtered and coughed its last gasp. A long wheezing sigh from under the bonnet announced its demise.

Sitting behind the wheel, Noemi stared blankly at the ransacked shop in front of her, pondering whether traveling to *any* city in search of sanctuary was wise.

She remained motionless, until a loud pounding jolted her back to the moment to see an agitated Santino, his gaze swinging back and forth between her window and his car.

Noemi rolled down the window. "What's wrong? Are the girls hurt?"

"N-No," Santino stammered. "It's Chiara—"

"God, no," Noemi broke in, fearful the virus had reared its head again. "Please, don't tell me she has relapsed."

"No, it's not that… she took a bullet—"

The word *bullet* propelled Noemi out of the truck and across the tarmac before Santino could finish his sentence.

Chasing after Noemi, Santino shouted, "She's slowed the bleeding, but we need to remove the bullet."

Seeing Chiara's blood-soaked blouse cinched tightly around the wound, Noemi instructed Santino to, "Check the back of the truck for a first-aid kit. I can patch it up until we get to Florence and proper medical attention."

Santino stopped in his tracks. "Where do you think all these cars were going, Noemi? My guess is they were turned back by the Florentine police. I doubt they are granting anyone entry into the city."

"We've no time to debate the issue, Santino." Noemi pointed at her friend's leg. "Your wife is losing blood. Surely, they would not turn us away."

"Are you willing to bet my wife's life on it? What if there's a huge queue of cars trying to get in. I am not prepared to take that chance. Any delay could be fatal."

"What do you suggest?" Noemi demanded.

"I have family nearby. I am sure we can find help there. Now, please stop arguing and climb in."

"Not until I've checked this wound. The first aid kit… scoot." Noemi's tone brooked no discussion.

Treating Chiara, who was slipping in and out of consciousness, as best she could, especially in such an unsterile environment, Noemi cleaned and packed the wound, bandaging it firmly.

Worried about the blood loss, she checked Chiara's radial pulse to get a base line, then her pedal pulse. The latter was thready, but Chiara's foot remained a reasonably healthy colour, which gave Noemi hope.

Rinsing her hands under a convenient tap, she nodded at the truck. "What about the truck and, more importantly, the cargo in the back?"

"If we lose it, we lose it. Otherwise, I am sure Joseppi's boys can take care of it. Who's going to bother looking in a truck with a bullet riddled cow on its side?"

The Petrea farm sat outside San Fedele. To Noemi, it was the epitome of a gypsy compound. Tractors and old trucks spread across the property, along with any number of goats and chickens.

Santino had not seen his cousin, Joseppi, since Santino and Chiara's nuptials. By family tradition, the couple's wedding ceremony was held at this farm. During the reception, the cousins had a disagreement, which led to a drunken brawl when an inebriated Joseppi expressed his disdain for Santino marrying an American on his land.

Sacrilege.

Santino alighted, stood next to his door, and blared the horn, yelling in Romani, "Petrea, get your ass out here."

The front door of the farm opened with a clatter, to reveal a man a few years older than Santino.

"Santino Bernardi. I thought I made it clear when I beat the crap out of you last time you were here that you are not welcome back."

"I've no time for your grievances, Joseppi. Chiara's been shot and I need your help."

Joseppi Petrea was a family man first, and a bellicose blowhard second, even if the woman in question was not *of the blood*.

"Well, don't stand there gawping at me like I've grown two heads, fool, bring her into my office. ***Now***."

Carrying Chiara, Santino followed Joseppi into what Noemi took to be a barn, leaving the latter to tend to the girls. Unbuckling the trio, Noemi hefted Sophia into her arms, instructing Nicoletta and Bianca to, "Hold hands and stay with me."

The lowing of cattle and bleating of sheep met the four as they approached a surprisingly clean, outwardly at least, stable, adjacent to the aged homestead.

Crossing the threshold, Noemi blinked furiously, squinting in the harsh light.

Bianca's hand shot up to shield her eyes from the glare, as she gave a delighted squeal, "Ohhhh, Mama, they are hidin' a spaceship in here."

True enough, the interior of the barn was lined in chrome and reflected the powerful overhead lights.

As Noemi's vision adjusted, the ramshackle barn complete with dilapidated stables or antiquated equipment, she expected to see, turned out to be a modern and immaculate veterinary clinic.

Santino lowered his wife onto a table, allowing the one called Joseppi to examine the wound.

Wheeling his stool to a nearby cabinet, searching for a pair of forceps, Joseppi asked, "Who treated the gunshot? No chance it was you, cousin."

Never the shy retiring type, for once, Noemi felt she ought not to intervene until introduced formally.

Spying her expression, Santino did the honours, "She did. This is Noemi Ricci."

Without looking at their new guest, Joseppi barked, "You have medical training?"

"Emergency medical training, sir," Noemi chastised herself inwardly for addressing the man as such. Not even her husband had earned that.

"Looks like you did a good enough job to save her life… ah… there they are," he found the missing surgical forceps, and gathered the rest of his gear.

Spinning on the chair, Joseppi addressed Noemi, "Care to give me a hand? If I have to depend on this lout, she is apt to need her leg amputated." He sneered at Santino.

"I sure as hell hope you plan to sterilise that equipment and wash your hands before using them on Chiara," Noemi snorted as Joseppi closed the drawer.

The man retaliated, his tone heavy with sarcasm, "Actually, no, I thought I'd use my rusty fishing knife. Would be a perfect test to prove whether God exists and wants her to live another day."

Sensing the stranger was about to flay him with vitriol… and probably question his sanity, Joseppi dropped the necessary instruments into an autoclave perched on a side bench.

"Now, Noemi Ricci, if you wish to help, wash up and put on a pair of gloves. I do not intend to save her leg, to lose her to some infection you passed because you were careless."

Joseppi indicated the industrial-size sink and box of surgical gloves alongside.

Fascinated, Noemi watched Joseppi's skilful fingers search for the fragment lodged in Chiara's leg. The device he used to locate it was one Noemi believed confined to medical books.

The Hirtz compass, commonly used by surgeons in World War I and long relegated to museum shelves, aided the veterinarian, who placed Noemi in charge of the suction machine to ensure the wound remained clear while he worked.

She marvelled at his dexterity, which equalled any of the chief surgeons with whom she was acquainted in Rome.

A talent wasted on farm animals, she mused, to hear Guilio chiding, *animals are people too.* Her mouth curved up slightly.

"Suction. Now," Joseppi's sharp instruction interrupted her contemplation.

"Might I ask a question, Doctor Petrea," curiosity getting the better of her. "Why a veterinarian?"

Without giving her a look, Joseppi replied, "Does being a vet instead of some overpriced surgeon, make me inferior?"

"No, I did not mean it that way. It's just with your touch—"

"Animals require tending to just as much as any human and are less likely to self-medicate or diagnose their own ailments."

Unexpectedly, he chuckled, "Besides, when your family are Romani, who has time to work in a hospital. I sew up enough wounds from knife fights and brawls."

There was a soft, stomach-churning squelch as he

removed what he judged to be a *Carcano* carbine rifle slug and dropped it into a dish on the adjacent rolling table. "No doubt somebody's great-grandfather's war trophy," he observed, matter-of-factly,

Intrigued by the extent of his guest's ability, he asked Noemi, "Can I trust you to suture the wound?"

Glancing between the bullet hole, the older man, and the array of instruments, she shrugged and threaded a needle with absorbable suture to stitch the internal laceration, impressing Joseppi with her knowledge.

Once closed, Noemi used a non-absorbable thread to seal the large puncture in poor Chiara's skin. While not necessarily as neat as his handiwork, Joseppi approved of her effort, and on closer inspection, the veterinarian rewarded Noemi with a "Not bad."

About to dispose of the needle, Noemi was stopped by Joseppi. "Not so fast. I'm not sure whether you've heard the news, but our country is in a mess. *Everything* needs to be repurposed... for now, at least."

Startled, she placed the needle onto the same tray as the instruments, and watched Joseppi return everything to the autoclave.

Securing the machine's door, he said over his shoulder, to no one in particular, "Where are you going?"

"Florence," Noemi answered.

"Forget that." Joseppi peeled off his gloves, threw them in the bin, and washed his hands. "No one is allowed in, not even us peasants living a stone's throw from our glorious city."

"Where do you suggest, sir?" This time, *sir* did not taste as bitter.

"We do not have much," Joseppi leaned against the counter, drying his hands, "but you are welcome to stay for the time being. I could use an extra pair of hands and, if I remember rightly, that one stretched out on the table knows a thing or two about anatomy. Unless you're in a hurry to go nowhere in particular..." he left that dangling, assuming they were not stupid enough to decline his offer.

Noemi and Santino exchanged looks before Santino agreed, reiterating... "For the time being."

"Good, that's settled." Joseppi grinned. "Let's get you and those children sorted."

"Errr... Dr Petr—" Noemi started.

"Joseppi," he broke in.

"Joseppi," she amended. "We have something you may find useful. Food and medical supplies."

Joseppi's jaw dropped.

"We left a truckload of stuff at an Autogrill about thirty clicks from here."

"Are you daft?" he spat.

"We had no choice, the truck died," Santino appeased.

"Bah," Joseppi growled, and strode out of the barn, yelling, "Nehemiah, Manfri, fire up the tractor and go with these fools to where they abandoned their treasure trove."

The disarray at the service station was oddly comforting and Noemi breathed a sigh of relief when she spotted the Swiss-cheesed bovine awaiting their return.

Until she saw the open rear doors.

"Oh, God," Noemi squealed. "We've been robbed."

Her dash forwards was arrested when a box popped out of the truck to land on the ground with a dusty thud. Two more appeared in the same careless manner followed by a couple of small boys covered in dirt and mud, so alike they had to be brothers, if not twins.

"I told you, Dante," Noemi and Santino heard one of the boys exclaim. "Some stupid eejit left us all the food we'll ever need."

"What if they come back, Dario?"

"You kiddin'? Jus' look at the truck. They gotta be dead. Now, do as I tell ya. Pick up that box, and let's get goin'.'"

"But it's heavy," the one called Dante protested.

"Stop whinin' and hurry up."

"No, you carry it. I'm taking this one." Dante made a beeline for the smaller one.

"Nah'ah. I found the truck first, so it's my d'sision who carries what."

While the boys bickered, Noemi and Santino circled the truck, to materialise at opposite sides, catching the pair by surprise.

Dario threw up his fists ready to defend *their* find. Dante copied his brother's stance.

"Oh, my heavens, Santino," Noemi feigned terror. "How shall we ever defeat these two and get our stuff back?"

"Jus' try it, lady," Dario challenged fiercely. "It's ours. Best you scram afore we 'ave to get nasty."

Striving to mask her mirth at the boy's scowl, Noemi adopted the persuasive tone she used when trying to coax her own children. "While I should like to see you try, I have a better idea. How about we share it? There is enough in there for all of us."

"Like heck there is," Dario shot back, but there was the faintest hint of vacillation in his reply.

"Hmm," Noemi made a show of pondering his rebuttal. "There's quite a lot. Do you have a way of getting it all home?"

"We dun have a home," Dante whimpered forlornly. "Mama went to Heaven and papa runned away."

"Shuddup, Dante. I told you papa will be back really

quick. He promised," his brother yelled, but Dante was already crumpling to the ground, wailing at being abandoned by his parents.

Noemi's maternal instincts kicked in and, unable to help herself, scooped the distraught child into her arms. Head bent, Dario charged at her, prepared to intervene to protect his brother, to be thwarted by Santino who swept him up en route.

As Noemi comforted Dante, Dario battered Santino's chest and face with his small fists, trying to break free.

"You have some strength there, boy," Santino observed, easily avoiding the barrage of blows. Grabbing Dario's flailing fists with one hand, he continued, his tone calm but firm, "Hold your horses and listen for just a minute. How about you and your brother stay with us until your papa comes back?

"Might even show you some proper defensive moves you can use the next time to try to pull off a truck heist..." His expression was serious, but his eyes twinkled with amuse-ment as the lad's nose crinkled in solemn contemplation.

"And we can take all we need when papa comes?" Dario bartered.

"I promise," Santino smiled, as Joseppi's boys arrived with the tractor

"Now we've got that sorted, put those boxes back on the truck and hop in the car. I foresee three children back at the farm who will be excited to meet you."

S ince fleeing Rome and coming under the protection, of sorts, of Joseppi Petrea, life had changed beyond all recognition, and not only for Noemi and her friends. The world was sliding so far into chaos, Noemi feared it might never recover.

Powerless to control anything outside their own circle, they focused on what they *could* control.

First, a long-needed rest was prescribed by Joseppi, not only to allow Chiara to recuperate, who now had a bullet wound to contend with on top of her cracked ribs, but also because it was obvious to the affable vet, that they all needed time to de-stress. Second, Noemi and Chiara used this enforced breathing space to direct the unpacking of the truck.

The food was stocked in the farm's massive cellar, while the equipment and medication was inventoried and stored in the surgical theatre.

In the middle of emptying the array of stuff, Noemi discovered they possessed not one case of the vaccine, but ten, and that each box contained five hundred doses.

Holding up one of the packages, she asked Chiara, "What should we do with them?"

Chiara sucked on her lip, rocking on the crutches as she pondered the question. "How comfortable are you with our research?"

"Meaning?"

"Thoughts on inoculating ourselves? We've already survived one strain of the virus, who's to say it has not already mutated?"

"As much as I believe in our scientific prowess, how about checking with Joseppi to see if he has a few rats to spare."

"No guts no glory," Chiara chuckled.

Global access to any form of television was lost within six weeks of the outbreak. Pockets of survivors relied on short-wave and ham radios to garner what sporadic information was transmitted.

Santino, especially, was saddened to hear that Noemi's prediction about creating an offshore *haven* had come true. Broadcasts from a handful of hardy reporters in the Libyan desert made for harrowing listening.

Death arrived either at the hands of desert marauders, who swooped in under the cover of darkness, raiding the camp's supplies, or as a result of the illness which had accompanied them across the Mediterranean. People who had trusted government propaganda and received their vaccinations, came to realise they offered minimal protection against the rapidly morphing variants of the virus.

As ever, when financial carrots are dangled, greed trumps safety.

The conclusion left for humanity: *Sanctuary was a lie!*

Despite their sorrow at the news regarding the loss of innocent lives in the desert, it proved to Noemi and Chiara that their due diligence was imperative with regards to the reliability of their serum.

It did not take long for the two women to cajole Joseppi into granting them a section of his barn to continue their experiments with the vaccines. This was accomplished by exposing rats to the blood of those who had perished from the contagion.

A resource not difficult to secure.

Word had spread through the surrounding villages about a doctor, of sorts, and his assistants were happy to take on the infected. This led to victims queueing at the farm gate in search of a miracle.

The oxygen masks had some success but, and regrettably, not for everyone.

Initially, after conducting autopsies to verify the cause of death and the effects of the illness, the dead were given proper burials at local cemeteries.

Eventually, as was the case around the rest of the world, bodies accumulated like firewood and mass cremations were the only solution. The pandemic cared nothing for the sensibilities of grieving families and friends.

Neither was the farm safe from the Grim Reaper's sickle.

Joseppi's youngest child, Sabina, had succumbed to the virus a few months previously, and his oldest, Nehemiah, was murdered by scavengers while hunting for more gauze and sutures.

The family discovered his battered body on the roadside not far from the Autogrill.

Periodically, even after Nehemiah's death, the inhabitants of the farm ventured to the service station to check whether anyone had responded to their notice concerning the twins.

Since the day Noemi had posted the message, the Autogrill's remaining front windowpane had become a makeshift bulletin-board for people seeking the missing.

Before long, the posts obscured the glass. Noemi and Chiara never failed to peruse the notes in case they recognised any of the names.

That the boys' father never returned for his sons gnawed at Noemi, who was unable to credit how *anyone* could abandon their children, let alone two such beautiful souls. Although, she had to concede he too could have fallen victim to the virus.

Fortunately for Dante and Dario, Joseppi and his wife, Rosella, despite suffering the loss of their own children, had no intention of letting the brothers fend for themselves.

Trial and error demonstrated that the vaccine, engineered at Ringtonwoth Pharmaceuticals and refined in their makeshift laboratory had a success rate of about thirty-seven percent.

Higher than the herd immunity of ten percent, it was below the levels required to defeat the virus, but *was* encouraging enough to warrant human testing, especially given all involved were dealing with the contamination on a daily basis.

The researchers, of course, were first.

Individually, both were hesitant and more than a little fearful to inject themselves, cognisant of the effects of preliminary versions, but neither expressed their concerns outwardly. Someone had to be a guinea pig and, as the architects of the vaccine, it was unfair to expect anyone else to take the risk.

Close monitoring and more testing followed, until the pair felt confident that the serum they had developed was safe enough to administer to any in the vicinity who requested it.

Noemi and Chiara hardly had a moment to call their own.

In the second year, the number of deaths began to dwindle, although Noemi and Chiara could not agree on whether this was because of the success of the vaccine, or the dramatic drop in the world's population as a whole.

The pair were not the only ones to notice the decrease in deaths. Those who had assumed control of their respective cities had, as was typical when war or disease *culled the herd*, deemed it imperative to initiate programs aimed at repopulation.

Unfortunately, technology had suffered a catastrophic failure following the collapse of civilization leaving these same overseers to consult with a handful of scientists who claimed to be experts in genetic engineering.

In scenes resembling animals being taken to market, healthy males were transported between cities like breeding bulls to mate with equally healthy local females.

Sady, the result was the opposite of expectations.

Inexplicably, the number of women dying during childbirth or their offspring being stillborn, superseded the virus as the leading cause of death.

Yet again, the farm did not escape unscathed.

Two Years Later

Motionless, Noemi stared out over the gently undulating landscape. The last two years had been one long nightmare. Losing Giulio, her career, and her home. Being shot at, fleeing Rome, battling the virus, being shot at again, then finding a haven of sorts with Joseppi and his family.

Setting up a clinic, helping the locals, becoming part of a community, and feeling as though this could become home — a pinprick of light at the end of a very dark tunnel.

Now this!

"Why her?" she whispered to the air. "Yeah, she was a spitfire who didn't suffer fools gladly and, to be honest, could be a real bitch when she felt like it, but she didn't deserve this, nor did Santino and Nicoletta. How will they cope?"

For the first time since their arrival at the Petreas' farm, tears spilled down Noemi's cheeks and she made no effort to stop them. Where were they going to find the strength to keep going when death stalked them at every turn?

The tears kept coming, her vision fractured and reformed in shades of green and brown, and gold and blue. Reminiscent of a kaleidoscope... a tapestry of shadows and light. Constantly changing, mirroring the capricious life they now faced — tenuous, mercurial, and volatile.

Just when she thought they had grasped the picture, made some sense of the upheaval... it shifted.

In the curious hush which had descended on the farm, memories flickered through Noemi's head. Chiara and she, laughing at the children's antics while bemoaning the ruination of *another* set of clothes.

Honing their surgical skills under Joseppi's irascible tutelage. Hours listening to Rosella as she educated the pair in the various holistic remedies they were reduced to dispensing.

Chattering like magpies during the few breaks they snatched, usually taken on the weather-worn chairs of the Petreas' porch, sipping or, more likely inhaling, the richly brewed and still available coffee so loved by their hosts.

Evenings sharing stories around the bonfire, weather permitting, or snuggled up in the great kitchen of the farm, logs ablaze in the hearth, heady aromas of whatever Rosella was baking teasing their nostrils.

Never a dull moment.

Teasing Chiara and Santino for their unwavering devotion, their fiery passion which usually resulted in one of the kids sticking a finger down their throat in a gagging gesture, or one of the adults begging the couple to, "Get a room."

Flashes of happiness amidst the misery.

"Why her?" she repeated, scrubbing her damp face and steeling herself. Chiara's pregnancy, while a shock, was also a source of excitement. As though the new life growing inside her was a symbol of hope for a brighter future.

The women of the group knew the dangers associated with childbirth. All three had witnessed enough fatalities in the adjacent neighbourhoods not to become complacent.

The need for midwives did not abate because of the pandemic, in fact once the first phase had run its course, the rate of pregnancies had increased... to the delight of the powers that be.

This did not, however, equate to straightforward births. Lack of hospitals, doctors, surgeons, and sterile centres of any kind heightened the risks to both mother and babe.

Chiara was no fool, she knew the risks, but trusted in her own health, the vaccine she and Noemi had created and tested rigorously, and God.

"I have to believe," she had admitted to an incredulous Noemi shortly after her pregnancy was confirmed. "It is part of who I am, who Santino is. Apart from our little family, my faith is about all I have left."

Wisely, Noemi had kept her counsel. Whatever got her friend through the night was all right by her.

"Some use you were," she vented her spleen to the heavens. "Couldn't let us keep her, could you? You do know this will kill Santino, and then where will Nicoletta be? She's barely five and has already seen too much. Honestly, you deities are a pack of selfish despots."

Grumbling ominously under her breath, Noemi straightened her shoulders and turned her back on the beautiful landscape, racking her brain for words, any words, which might offer a modicum of comfort to a family who, in the blink of an eye, had gone from four to two.

10

Chiara's death left a hole in the family no one could find a way to fill. Santino lost himself in training the children, despite their tender years, in the art of self-defence.

He carved blunted, wooden knives for the older four. Given, Sophia, a toddler, struggled to get her spoon to her mouth, the last thing anyone needed was for her to be wielding a weapon. While they could not inflict serious harm on one another, they still found a way to leave dark welts on their opponents.

Noemi struggled to move on from the loss of her best friend, shouldering the blame for being unable to save Chiara and, gradually, retreated from the rest of the household, except Bianca and Sophia. Her daughters became her lifeline, and she clung to them both mentally and physically, the latter manifesting in fierce and protracted hugs, refusing to release them until the girls yelled for Uncle Santi.

She no longer assisted Joseppi in the clinic. Her hatred for the virus extended to anyone who dared appear at the door begging for help.

One morning, perhaps six months later, a loud rumbling stirred the residents inside the house from a quiet breakfast and brought them to the porch. Three, huge, black SUVs bearing the flag of Florence came to a halt at the gate.

A short, slender man, dressed in what looked like a hastily altered military uniform, embroidered with a carabinieri insignia… a confusing combination… alighted from the lead vehicle, carrying a roll of parchment.

Unfurling it, he announced in an overly pompous voice, "By order of the Condottiero Glorioso of Firenze. For the welfare of its citizens, all food and medical supplies are to be surrendered to the bearer of this decree. Failure to do so will be considered an act of treason, punishable by the seizure of property and imprisonment without trial. You have fifteen minutes to comply."

Letting the scroll coil up, he was about to stuff it into his coat pocket when a gaunt, careworn-looking woman approached, hands clasped behind her back.

She did not appear to present any risk but, at almost the same height, forced him to look her in the eye.

"What do you want?" he demanded.

"I am sorry, sir," Noemi replied in far more demure tones than she usually employed. "I am sure you can understand our hesitation to hand everything we own to you. Please allow me to read the missive, so I can judge its authenticity, and be assured it does indeed hold the Condottiero Glorioso's seal."

The officer huffed. He had better things to do than deal with these country bumpkins but, if it meant concluding *negotiations* quickly, so be it.

"Fine." He glowered. "If it expedites proceedings, here."

He approached her, holding out the scroll, stunned by the speed with which she grabbed his sleeve, and hauled him forwards onto the blade which appeared, seemingly, out of nowhere. The scream she emitted was blood-curdling.

Before he could repel her attack, cold steel speared his throat from front to back, cutting off his terrified shriek. Blood spurted out in warm jets, drenching Noemi who, without batting an eyelid, bisected his neck, cleaving his head from his shoulders.

The captain's subordinates leapt from their vehicles, shocked gazes fixed on the insane banshee, who stood motionless before them, their commanding officer's head dangling from her bloodied hand. As, instinctively, fingers gripped holstered pistols, they were confronted by Santino and Joseppi.

Santino — his own pistol already drawn, while his cousin levelled his double-barrelled shotgun — warned, "Unless you plan to join your foolhardy captain in the afterlife, I suggest you beat a hasty retreat back to that cesspit you call Florence."

The meagre cohort did not need to be told twice. They didn't get paid enough for this shit. Looking at each other, they shrugged, hopped back into their respective trucks, and fled.

Once certain they had left, Santino turned to Noemi. Her eyes were glassy, her expression distant. He spoke her name and shook her by the shoulder, but she did not react.

This was the second life Noemi had taken but, this time, it felt… easier? She acknowledged it was a reckless and unnecessary act of violence. So, why did it leave her with a strange sense of euphoria?

Has all this death stolen the last of my humanity?

Clutching the head by its hair like a war trophy, she stalked back to the house, instructing everyone to, "Pack up. We cannot stay here."

Hurriedly, but methodically, Santino and Noemi loaded the minibus — appropriated the previous year from the service station because as Chiara had pointed out, their little hatchback could not seat eight — with provisions.

Joseppi pulled up beside them in a large truck to which was hitched a caravan.

Rolling down his window, he said, "I figured this day would arrive. Mind if we come along for the ride?"

At last, guilt hit Noemi, not for taking the soldier's life, but for compelling the Petreas to abandon their home.

"I've cost you everything, Joseppi. I'm so sorry."

"Nonsense, girl." Joseppi grinned wryly. "You did what you had to do. I would have done the same."

Joseppi shouted at Santino, "Hey, boy, you reckon that little toy of yours can pull one of these?" He jerked his thumb over his shoulder at the caravan. "It'll be a squeeze trying to sleep seven in that bone rattler."

Santino and Noemi looked at each other. Neither had thought about their sleeping arrangements, but spending the rest of their lives with five children in a minibus was not an attractive prospect.

"Don't just stand there gawking at each other. I have another caravan big enough for all of you. Last I looked, it was in decent shape, though I can't promise you won't find the odd rodent using it as a squat."

Climbing down from the truck, Joseppi stood on the step of the minibus and directed them through a field to where, concealed in an old olive grove, sat a compact, blue caravan.

When it came into view, Noemi's second thought was, *beggars can't be choosers...* her first was not repeatable. The van looked as though it had been tucked in this quiet corner since the fall of Rome.

The shell was rusty and discoloured, and the tires flattened, but a peek around the door revealed a surprisingly clean and tidy interior, complete with a kitchen, two bedrooms, and a fold out set of bunks where the dining table sat.

"Like I said, cosy and comfortable," Joseppi's cheery tone was reminiscent of a caravan salesman.

"Nowhere near the size of yours," Santino protested.

Unsure why the situation resembled two camel traders haggling, Noemi bit back a giggle, suspecting neither cousin would appreciate the humour.

Must be in the blood.

"And *you* do not have near the number of kids either, cousin," Joseppi countered.

Momentarily, silence fell between them.

Joseppi blew an impatient huff. "Look, all it needs is a good scrub inside and out, some fresh curtains and, voila, new caravan."

"I suppose," Santino relented. "How do you propose we move this tetanus dispensary? I don't think there's a chance in hell those tires will ever be round again."

Ever the magician, Joseppi produced two good tires, and left Santino to change the old ones.

By the time Noemi and Santino returned to the house, caravan in tow, the last of the Petreas' children was climbing into the back of the truck, making a space between the mountain of supplies Joseppi and Rosella had crammed in.

Like Moses leading the Israelites through the wilderness, they began their exodus across the Italian peninsula.

To everyone's amazement, Noemi had a particular destination in mind. Through the back roads heading south, the group drove towards Rome.

11

A trip which, before the collapse of civilisation, took about four hours, now took more than two days, and required them to learn to barter for fuel and other necessities on the fly.

Pulling into a rest area on the outskirts of Rome, Noemi hopped out of the minivan and flagged Joseppi to pull up alongside.

He rolled down his window, Noemi saying before he could ask… "To set up camp here."

He nodded slowly, something in her voice prompting his next words, "No problem, but that sounds like you have other plans."

Staring at the hazy outline of the Eternal City, Noemi replied, "I need to apologise to someone for leaving them there."

She returned her gaze to Joseppi. "Can I entrust the girls to you, in case—"

"Do not finish that question, Noemi Ricci," Rosella expostulated from the passenger seat, then softened her tone,

"We'll help Santino watch over your precious daughters while you do whatever it is you need to do."

Noemi forced a smile. "I appreciate that, Rosella."

"*Di niente*, and don't hesitate to check out the shops… you know, in case you come across any which happen to be open," she paused, "and still stocked. I could do with a new dress or two, and some decent shoes." She shot her husband an impish grin.

Joseppi rolled his eyes and gave a very husbandly long-suffering sigh. "How long do you expect this *shopping spree* to take?"

"I should be back by tomorrow evening, maybe the day after. I want to check whether I can salvage anything from my home."

"Is it worth it? It's been nigh on three years. It may well have new owners." Santino, approaching from behind, interjected.

Noemi twisted to lean on the door of Joseppi's truck, swallowing a chuckle at the sight of Santino toting Nicoletta with Sophia and Bianca clutching his trouser leg.

"No harm in looking," she infused a positive note into her reply. In truth, she doubted anything remained of their possessions. Her house was probably overrun with rats… or worse… squatters.

Noemi shifted her attention to her older daughter. "I need you to be a good girl and help Uncle Santi and the Petreas with the children. Can you do that for me, poppet?"

"Noooooo…" the child wailed, turning on the waterworks. "I-I w-wanna go h-home and see papa."

"Darling, I would love to take you with me, but this is something mama needs to do by herself first, to make sure everything is safe before you come with. When you're older—"

"No, Mama," Bianca snapped, jutting out her chin defiantly.

The gesture was exactly Guilio eliciting an unexpected stab of grief in his widow.

"I. Am. Older," Bianca declared, scrubbing the tears from her eyes with clenched fists. "'Sides, if you find lots of stuff, you'll need help to carry it."

Noemi's heart cracked hearing her daughter reason like an adult.

It's unfair her childhood was stolen from her so young.

All eyes focused on the mother to see her response, which surprised everyone.

"You promise to do *exactly* as I tell you?"

"Yes, Mama…" Bianca edged closer to her mother, "…and I will make sure *no one* sneaks up behind us," she promised. "Even if I have to walk backwards."

Noemi could not help but smile… *out of the mouths of babes.*

At the behest of the other three adults, Noemi was persuaded to take the minibus.

"Doesn't need to stay hitched to the van," Santino justified their decision. "It's not like we can generate power anyway. Candles for light and there's enough cold cuts to keep us going."

"I've got extra rations," Rosella interjected. "Go." She flapped her hands at Noemi. "We are perfectly capable of looking after ourselves. You're the one heading into unknown territory."

"Nuh-uh," Noemi refuted. "It's my home."

Rosella arched a sceptical brow. "You reckon? I'll ask you that again when you get back."

Conceding it was a losing battle, Noemi capitulated, secretly relieved she could take the minibus.

Walking into Rome with Bianca was not an attractive prospect, aware her daughter would be fed up before they had covered a fifth of the distance.

More importantly, not only could she fit far more in the vehicle than she could carry, but also, it offered the means for a quick getaway should that prove necessary.

At dusk, food, blankets, and matches stowed in the minibus and Bianca buckled in, Noemi set off. While her friends had vetoed the idea of heading to Rome under cover of darkness, Noemi argued that it was the safer option.

The roads were eerily quiet. The dull roar of traffic and constant blare of sirens, synonymous with Rome was missing, the lack of noise unnerving.

Bianca, who did not remember much about their life before they fled the city, was not in the slightest perturbed and entertained her mother with a selection of nursery rhymes, encouraging Noemi to join in if there was a chorus.

As a distraction, it worked pretty well, until they reached the heart of Rome.

During the last three years, communication with anyone beyond their small community was almost impossible. The notice board at the service station had become more of a news service than the handful of shortwave radios still in operation. Information was sporadic and unreliable. Everyone had an agenda, and no one knew who or what to trust. For once, ignorance was bliss.

Now, Noemi wished she had listened to the occasional broadcasts; the devastation of her beloved city was difficult to comprehend. The previously elegant streets resembled slums, the beautiful architecture despoiled, probably beyond repair. Houses and businesses abandoned.

She counted scarcely a single undamaged window or door.

How were people surviving?

Carefully nosing the minibus along the roads to Trastevere and their home, Noemi questioned her sanity.

Santino was right, this is a complete waste of time.

Yet, she pushed on. Even if their home was ruined, she needed to see for herself.

Glinting in the moonlight, vehicles, of sorts, had been cobbled together, using whatever materials available, reminding Noemi of Steampunk, the design-style most easily described as Victorian-era industrial engineering meets fantasy fiction.

It seemed oddly ironic given the trend was inspired by the notion of a post-apocalyptic world.

Humans, she mused while concentrating on not ploughing into any of the bizarre contraptions as she sought a parking space, *will always find a way to surmount the obstacles thrown at them.*

Coming to a stop in front of their former home, Noemi glanced at her watch. It was almost midnight. Why she had done so had escaped her, it was not as though Giulio was waiting anxiously for her to return home; set to lecture her for working too late at the lab… as always.

Hands resting idly on the steering wheel, she listened to Bianca's soft snores, keenly aware, despite her daughter's enthusiasm, she could not have walked the distance… but blessed her aspiration. It boded well for her future.

To the deity she had yet to forgive for Chiara's premature death, she murmured, "Thank you, God, for convincing me to trust someone else's advice."

That was where her appreciation ended.

Gripping a torch, Noemi alighted quietly, inhaled a long slow breath, and took stock of her surroundings, registering the deplorable state of the houses on the street. Doors hung off their hinges or had been removed altogether. Splintered fragments of furniture and scraps of rotting material, which could be anything from clothes to curtains, littered the pavement.

Reappraising man's ingenuity concerning the vehicles she had just passed, she tacked on, *and will destroy anything they don't need, without a second's thought.*

Ascending the steps to her former home, a loud rustling within made her pause. Swinging the flashlight, she saw nothing but the tattered remnants of her once prized dwelling.

Presuming it was an animal scrounging for food, she took extra care to not spook it as she crept in.

Noemi was picking her way through the debris, when Bianca's voice reached her from the door.

"Mama, are you in here?"

Noemi was astounded. *So much for child-proof safety harnesses.* Nor did she imagine Bianca would think to leave the safety of the minibus in the middle of the night... forgetting her daughter was seven going on eighteen.

She turned to answer, at the same instant as two shadows rushed out of the inky depths of the house. The beam from her torch caught the flicker of something metallic... and large.

Before Noemi could scream a warning to Bianca, she heard her daughter's shocked yelp when the figures barrelled into her. The one holding the metal object bolted outside, the other had, seemingly, vanished.

Instead of the deafening bawl she expected, and prayed, to hear, Noemi was dumbstruck when her angelic-looking daughter unleashed a torrent of obscenities — mostly mispronounced, as befitted a seventy-year-old drunken sailor, not a seven-year-old girl — to the accompaniment of fists battering flesh.

A reedy voice piped up, "Antonio, get murder mittens off me."

"Dammit, Angelo, just kick the stupid cat and get out of there," an impatient treble replied.

Bianca hissed, "You better not hit a girl. Unless you *want* me to slay you."

"Antonio, heeeeeeelp," genuine panic underscored the boy's plea.

Noemi hauled her daughter off the bedraggled… and now bruised… boy and placed a firm foot on his chest pinning him to the floor. She squinted through the door at the other urchin who was clutching what Noemi recognised to be Giulio's ceremonial blade, a little worse for wear after three years of neglect.

"Drop the sword boy. It. Is. Not. Yours." The ominous note in Noemi's voice fell on deaf ears.

"Finder's keepers, lady. 'Sides I don't see your name on it."

"How do you know?"

That shut him up, and the one called Angelo cackled a rasping laugh.

"Dun't make any difference whose name's on it… he can't read a lick anyway."

Noemi made the mistake of shifting her foot.

Slippery as an eel, Angelo was on his feet and darting after Antonio. The pair struggled to get through the narrow gate and in the scuffle, there was a dissonant clang accompanied by a lot of shuffling in the leaves.

"Never mind that bloody thing," Angelo, emboldened by his escape, exhorted. "Come on, it's not worth it. Eh, but that little cat had claws. Who'da thunk it?"

"Who cares about her, I've lost a good weapon," the plaintive whine of Antonio floated back to Noemi who had shot out of the door in hot pursuit.

Too late, they had scarpered.

Biting her tongue on some choice expletives, she stomped back into the house, the heel of her boot kicking something. Bending, she rummaged in the darkness, her fingers closing around a solid object. Giulio's sword.

Relief washed over her, and she tilted her head to smile upwards. "Ok, that makes us even."

Not wishing to linger in the pitch-dark house any longer than necessary, Noemi began to gather whatever might prove useful, stacking everything at the front door. Bianca did what she could to help, stoically ignoring the broken toys and games strewn around the shambles which was once her bedroom.

In the wreckage of her study, Noemi discovered that although her collection of medical and pharmaceutical books were scattered all over the floor, they had survived relatively intact. *Clearly, knowledge was deemed worthless... blinkered fools. Sad to think how many people died because they overlooked the value of these.*

The tap of light feet approaching reminded Noemi that before the world went to hell in a hand basket, this room was strictly off limits to Bianca and any of her friends.

Sensitive research and small children intent on playing with anything they could get their hands on was not a good mix.

A concern rendered null and void in a heartbeat. Her lip curled, *how quickly one's priorities change.*

"Mama," the tired voice yawned, "are papa's picture books in here, too? You know, the ones with the pretty old buildings in them?"

Giulio's fascination with architecture had surprised Noemi, as had his insistence on sharing the fascination with his firstborn.

The darkness concealed Noemi's sad smile. "How about we try to find them?"

Satisfied they had retrieved everything they could, the two hauled their treasures to the minibus, and stashed them in the back. Once in their seats, Noemi locked the doors, and wrapped the seatbelts around the armrests to prevent anyone breaking in.

Secure, and relatively comfortable, they succumbed to sleep.

Noemi awoke before Bianca. Rubbing her eyes, she took one last look at remains of their house, made even more depressing by the mocking promise of a new day.

Turning the key in the ignition, she listened to the purr of the engine warming up, then drove to their last destination before leaving the city… the Protestant Cemetery and her husband's grave.

They arrived as the sun breached the horizon. Parking near the Pyramid of Cestius, Noemi selected some of the food they had brought, along with a blanket.

Locating a suitable spot, she spread out the blanket and set up a small picnic then fetched her daughter from her seat.

Yawning and stretching, Bianca asked drowsily, "Are we there yet?"

"Not quite, poppet," Noemi replied, "we need to see your papa before we leave."

"Papa?" Bianca exclaimed, confused until she saw the array of headstones. "Oh."

Taking Bianca's hand, Noemi led her to where she recalled burying Giulio. Given the passage of time, the lack of a tombstone, and her hope that no one had disturbed his resting place, it was a best guess.

Lost in thought, they stood together contemplating the bare earth then returned to the blanket, made themselves comfortable and ate without talking. The dawn chorus tuning up added a curious normality to their scratch meal.

Full, Bianca wandered back to where... if her mother's memory was to be trusted... her father was buried.

She kicked at the grass. "I don't know if you can hear me, Papa, but I hope you can. You would be pleased at how tall I have grown since the last time you saw me.

"I've worked really hard to help Mama take care of Sophia and Nicoletta, especially after Nicoletta's Mama and her baby brother went to Heaven."

Noemi followed but kept her distance and stayed quiet, aware her daughter needed these few moments more than she did.

"I don't know much else, Papa," Bianca was about to end her conversation, when a thought struck her. "Oh, yeah, I have your picture books. I wanted to take them to teach Sophia and Nicoletta about them, and maybe go see them when we get grown up.

"If those two stinky boys, Mama found — I know you wouldn't like them 'cos they are really stinky — are nicer to us girls, I might take them too. It's like Mama says, feral animals make bad house pets, and I don't think they can ever be house-broked.

"Okay, Papa, we should get back to Uncle Santi. I promise to visit next time we're here."

Without acknowledging her mother, Bianca trudged back to the minivan and climbed in, while Noemi packed up the impromptu picnic.

Bianca looked out the window. "It's so sad that Papa has no rock to mark his grave, like the others."

"On the contrary, poppet," Noemi, settled behind the wheel, smiled at her daughter through the mirror, and pointed to the pyramid of Cestius. "He has the largest marker in the cemetery."

This made Bianca very happy.

"Ready to go back to the others?"

"Yes, Mama."

12

Noemi cruised to a stop next to the caravan to see Santino chasing Nicoletta and Sophia, who were half-dressed and giggling hysterically, as they dodged his clutches.

"I told you two to finish getting dressed," Noemi heard the poor man yelling, which had zero effect.

Unbuckling Bianca, she said, "Run around the other side of the caravan and help Uncle Santi."

"You bet, Mama," Bianca replied eagerly.

It did not take her long to corral the whooping demons, herding them into the caravan.

Santino leant against the side of the trailer, gulping in lungfuls of air, trying to catch his breath. At the sound of dried leaves being crunched underfoot, he looked up to see Noemi grinning as she examined the overturned wash tub.

He raised his palm to stave off the ridicule he knew was coming. "Don't say a word, woman. I thought I would be helpful and have them take a bath before you got back. Somehow, they found the only patch of mud in a hundred kilometres."

Noemi made no attempt to mask her mirth. "So, who jumped first?"

"If I told you, you'd say I deserved it for raising a hellion."

Spying a vehicle, not there when she left, Noemi asked, "Who are the new neighbours?"

"No idea. They arrived sometime during the night. Haven't seen hide nor hair of them. Mind, I do like the tent setup on top of their wagon. Very useful."

"Are you kidding? Knowing our lot, they'd roll out of the flaps and fall to their deaths, sound asleep no less."

"You worry too much, Noemi Ricci. We both know they would bounce as soon as they hit the ground."

As their laughter rang around the little encampment, they noticed the window of the newcomers' tent roll up with a snap, then drop back just as quickly.

"My guess is they feel there is safety in numbers, but are too scared to be sociable," Santino remarked at Noemi's quizzical brow.

"Let's give the rabbits some time to see if they dare venture out of their hutch."

Although Rosella laid on a substantial lunch, hoping the new arrivals might join them, the latter did not appear. Not even the bright chatter of the extended family group was enough to entice them out.

Unwilling to force the issue, the others carried on as usual. After everyone had eaten their fill, Rosella cleared the table, keeping a watchful eye on the children who had a habit of sneaking off to avoid what they deemed a total waste of time. School.

Not a qualified teacher, Rosella had homeschooled her

older children before the end of civilisation and refused to allow the younger ones to go uneducated. Maths, history, literature… nothing was ignored.

Even science was included in their improvised curriculum, although Rosella pressed the one with a doctorate in pharmacology into service to teach that subject.

Checking the time on her watch, Noemi realised, if she did not hurry, *she* would be the one being punished for being late to class.

Her nose buried in her notes, she came out of the caravan and nearly broke her neck tripping over some jugs of water and a few canned goods someone had placed on the step.

There was only one person absent-minded enough to leave it there. "Joseppi Petrea. Are you trying to kill me?" she bellowed.

The vet came around the corner. "Wow… I'm not in Rome. What are you bawling about?"

"This." She pointed at the offending items. "Due warning next time… you know a quick heads-up. Why you thought we did not have enough water al—"

"I didn't put them there," Joseppi objected. "Maybe it was Santino."

"Again, why? We have plenty of water."

A sharp movement caught their eyes, and both looked across at the newcomers' vehicle in time to see the tent flap close.

Noemi pondered, "D'you suppose it's from them?"

"Could be their way of saying hello, or at least an offering so we don't chase 'em off."

Staring at the tent, Noemi said, "Do me a favour and have your wife…" she handed him her notes, "…fill in for me. I think it's time I introduced myself."

He shot her a wary look, "Do you think that's a good idea?"

"One way to find out."

Joseppi gave Noemi's lesson notes a cursory glance. "Ya know, I am a trained medical professional and know a thing or two about chemistry and biology. I am fairly certain I can—"

"Can what? Scare the children to death with stories of conjoined lambs, with pictures no less?"

"Well, they should be aware of what could happen?"

"Hardly. The world is terrifying enough. They *do not* need any more help from you. Now hurry up, before we both get in trouble from your wife for disrupting her lessons."

Cautiously, Noemi approached the SUV. She contemplated climbing up the ladder to the tent, but thought better of it, opting to hail the occupants, "Hello there, anybody home?"

Slowly, the tent's zip slid upwards. A head, sporting a shock of shaggy dark-brown hair and matching bushy beard, pushed through the opening. Drained of colour, the stranger's face appeared fatigued.

His reply was more fearful plea, than courteous greeting, "Please, ma'am, do not send us away. If the water and food are not enough—"

"Why would I send you packing? Are you planning to lull me into a false sense of security, then steal everything we own?"

His expression morphed from weary to startled. "Never, ma'am. But we have seen things—"

"Haven't we all? Look, rather than me getting a stiff neck, perhaps we can continue this conversation at eye level. Come down, grab your stuff from the front of my caravan, and meet the rest of us.

After a quick word with someone behind him, he nodded at Noemi. Shortly thereafter, two people descended from the tent and introduced themselves. He was a carpenter by trade, his wife a seamstress.

This marked a new beginning. As the disparate band roamed the countryside, in search of somewhere safe to establish a more permanent base, the handful of hardy survivors became a community, their numbers increasing when joined by other like-minded individuals.

A sense of optimism permeated the group and, for the first time since the global crisis struck, their future did not look not quite so bleak.

Before their nomadic existence began, however, there were two more Noemi felt inclined to collect.

The next day, in the pale grey of the pre-dawn, Noemi pointed the minibus at Rome, grateful her daughters were in safe hands for the duration of her absence, which, she hoped to be brief.

Evasive about the nature of her mission, Noemi knew, by the time Bianca finished regaling the group with her adventures in the city as her mama's bodyguard, they would guess the reason behind her return.

As she approached the city's invisible boundary, Noemi was astonished to see a checkpoint, not there yesterday morning. A guard clad in army fatigues approached her vehicle, his friendly grin when he indicated she needed to roll down her window, another surprise.

"Buongiorno, signora. May I see your identification, please," his tone as welcoming as his cheerful countenance.

"This is new," Noemi observed, digging for her driving license.

Without breaking his smile, he explained, "The tribunal has concluded that we in the Eternal City, be ever vigilant against the barbarian hordes which surround us."

The statement struck Noemi as odd, not least that it sounded scripted. She wondered whether a centurion, millennia ago, had expressed the same rehearsed and oft repeated edict to other travellers attempting to gain entry. Banishing the image of the man in front of her in the attire of a Roman legionary complete with red-crested helmet, she handed over her license.

He studied it, and his brow furrowed, his demeanour sobering. "Ma'am, this is an outdated form of identification."

Glancing around to verify they were alone, he continued quietly, "I will permit you access, if you assure me, you have already visited the civilian offices to apply for a new citizenship card."

The eyes holding hers were nervous, both knew that by authorising her admittance into the city, without correct documentation, he chanced a severe reprimand, although proving she was a resident of Rome had created a sense of camaraderie between them.

"Oh, yes, sir. They were experiencing problems with their printer at the time, which should be rectified by week's end," she lied blithely.

His features relaxed. "Ahhh, yes. I am cognisant of the administrative issues facing the recently installed government."

He took a step away from the vehicle and saluted. "Have a great day and be careful. As you know, portions of our city remain unsafe for a woman on her own."

Smiling, Noemi waved a goodbye. "Aye, you do not need to warn me twice."

Unsure where to search for the two boys, Noemi decided her old neighbourhood was probably a good starting point.

She scoured the narrow, winding streets of Trastevere on foot and, where possible, in the van, until she questioned whether this was a fool's errand, because all she found was a horde of rats hunting for food.

Debating the worth of one last circuit, she heard the clatter of metal. About to dismiss it as said rodents scrabbling through rubbish, she saw a can hurtle through the air, at the same instant as a child shot out of a side street.

Noemi slammed on her brakes to avoid hitting the boy, whom she recognised as Angelo, amazed at how nimbly he avoided her vehicle and the projectile. A far cry from when he was pinned under Bianca, getting soundly pummelled. She chuckled softly.

A much taller, and to Noemi unidentified, boy tumbled out of the same street, Antonio clinging to his back like a limpet, thrashing him about the head with a stick.

Angelo yelled, "Jump."

Noemi watched Antonio catapult off his quarry in a backflip an Olympic gymnast would be proud of, to land on his feet like a cat. In the same fluid movement, he bent to grab something from the street.

Noemi realised the two must have a signal because at the same moment and with no obvious warning, Angelo ducked. A large rock sailed over his head to nail the third boy in the back causing him to stumble and skid along the cobbles. He caught his footing and skedaddled.

Angelo crowed, "If you want another ass kicking, Louis, try stealing from us again."

Noemi opened the minibus door, preparing to speak to

the boys in hopes of persuading them to go with her when her elbow caught the horn. The discordant honk echoed around the empty buildings.

The two boys spun around. Seeing Noemi, Antonio squawked, "Run! It is that crazy woman from the other night!"

"What the hell does she want?" Angelo quizzed.

"Who knows, but I'm not hanging about to find out."

They split up and fled in opposite directions, vanishing before she could reach them.

Instead of giving chase, Noemi opted to investigate the street to understand what they were fighting over, discovering a tattered bag of mealy apples and some dented cans of peas.

Noemi was saddened that the pair was reduced to eating garbage… let alone risk their lives to keep it.

Hopping into the minibus, she returned to her old home. Parking, she locked the vehicle, grabbed an old cloth bag, and walked into the heart of Trastevere, hoping one of the bakeries was still in business.

Noemi tried to ignore the sense of desolation pervading the streets as she passed unlit windows, plastered with *Going Out of Business* signs. Once an area bustling with tourists and locals alike, the silence was unnerving.

She exhaled a sigh of relief when she reached Antico Forno Alessia to find it still operating. Using traditional methods, this family-owned artisan bakery had supplied its customers with a daily selection of bread, pastries, pizza, and cakes for over a hundred and fifty years. More recently, their wood-fired oven meant the bakers could thumb their collective noses at the lack of gas and electricity.

The smoke coiling skywards suggested they continued to serve, although now the interior was illuminated by candles perched in wall sconces, creating the illusion the customer was stepping back in time to a more hospitable period.

The small bell above the door announced her entrance, and Noemi inhaled deeply, wanting to savour the rustic aroma of the artisan bread.

The scene triggered memories of when Giulio and she

started dating. A junior officer, Giulio had little money but was desperate to impress the young research assistant. She had lost count of the times the two shared a bottle of red wine and a loaf of bread.

A gruff voice disturbed a long-ago night spent with her husband, "Are you planning to buy something, Signora?" He paused and looked at his customer more closely. "Wait… Noemi Ricci as I live and breathe. Well, I never."

Noemi grinned. "Buongiorno, Nico. I thought you might have forgotten me, or worse, closed down altogether. I just happened to be passing through and wondered whether you had any panettone?"

"Forget my best customer…? Not a chance." He laughed, the wrinkles on his elderly face deepening. "In answer to your question, sadly no. We cannot get raisins for love nor money. No one is tending the vineyards anymore. It's so bad, the government is considering paying the farmers to return to the fields."

"Dang, that's a shame. Ok, what have you got?"

"Pane Toscano and ciriola," the latter being the ever-popular crusty, flame-shaped rolls.

Unsure what the boys would prefer, she said, "I'll have a loaf and a dozen rolls, if you have enough." She scanned the glass display cabinets whose contents were not as sparse as she expected. "Is that a crostata? Where did you get the cherries?"

"Giovanna has enough jars of preserved cherries to feed half the peninsula." Referring to his wife. "I promised never to complain about her hoarding again." Nico's face creased in amusement.

"I bet." Noemi joined in his laughter. "Gia ok?" She held her breath, hoping for an answer in the affirmative. No one dared ask about unseen loved ones anymore.

"She's fine, thank you. So far, we appear to have avoided

the worst of it. Right you are." Whistling, he put the delicious-looking selection into Noemi's bag.

"How much will that be?" She dug in her bag for money.

"I can't take euros," Nico stopped her before she handed over the cash. "Those worthless notes don't even make decent wallpaper. Everybody knows that…" He leant on the display case, arching his eyebrow at her, "…so why do you not?"

Noemi shrugged. "I've been out of the city for the last couple of years. We don't know what's going on anymore."

"Not necessarily a bad thing." Nico chuckled.

"Hmmm… maybe, maybe not." Noemi shrugged.

"Okay, do you have anything to barter with?"

Noemi considered that, then slid off her watch. "This any good?" she asked.

Nico weighed up the timepiece. It was Giulio's, an expensive Rolex. Noemi had given it to him on their fifth wedding anniversary. Keeping time no longer mattered, and if it got her some food, all the better.

"This is *very* good." Nico winked, adding another two loaves and four bottles of juice to her bag. "On the house."

Noemi forbore from mentioning that the watch could probably buy his business, never mind a few loaves, and thanked him.

"Don't be a stranger," he said as she collected her purchases.

"Can't promise." She smiled and pushed the door, the bell jingling merrily as the door swung open, then closed.

Retracing her steps, Noemi was outside her home in minutes, relieved to see the minibus had not been stripped for parts in her short absence.

Not prepared to take any chances, she ensured the doors were locked and looped the seat belts around the handles, as she had two nights ago.

Extracting a still warm roll from the bag, she munched it, watching the road for any movement. Tomorrow would bring another chance to contact the boys.

Following a far more restful sleep than she anticipated, Noemi coaxed her aching body out of the minibus and into her home. It was strange to walk through a place so familiar yet completely unrecognisable.

Nothing had changed since her previous visit but, in the early morning light, the disarray looked more… disheartening… sickening. That intruders had rifled through her personal belongings left a bitter taste in her mouth.

The drawers and cupboards were wrenched open, their contents either stolen or strewn about the floor. Surprisingly, most of her furniture was intact, if upskittled, but was covered in a thick layer of dust, and mould had claimed anything prone to getting damp.

She breathed in the musty air, assailed by a wave of melancholy. Her first home, her only home, once her pride and joy. Unbidden, it came to her that she was glad Giulio had not lived to witness such senseless and wholesale destruction.

The world was out of control.

Blinking back pesky tears, she straightened her shoulders, banished the emotion to the furthest recesses of her mind, and concentrated on what she could control.

In the daylight, Noemi was able to conduct a thorough and more methodical search of every room, packing the minibus with anything she had missed the first time around. This included several box-files containing papers and journals relating to her work at Ringtonwoth Pharmaceuticals.

One never knew when such information might be important.

She was closing the door of the van when the treble tones of Angelo and Antonio drifted along the street.

How do I handle this? she ruminated.

Trying to persuade two young lads to accompany her to an encampment sounded like the plot of a murder mystery, or an episode of some child trafficking documentary.

Even using food as a lure smacked of the child-catcher in Chitty Chitty Bang Bang. Noemi decided honesty was the best… and her only… policy.

She rounded the van, coming face to face with the pair.

"Oh no, not you again," Antonio groaned. "Can't yer mind yer own business?"

"I only want a quick word. Give me five minutes, and I'll give you some fresh crostata. If you aren't interested in what I say, you can go on your way, no hard feelings."

Antonio was about to reject this interfering old busybody's offer when Angelo sighed rapturously, "Crostata? Where did you find crostata?"

"I know Nico who owns Antico Forno Alessia. I bought some yesterday."

This got their attention. Three years after everything went to pot, Nico's baking was still legendary, his skill acclaimed far beyond Trastevere.

Wide-eyed, Angelo inched closer. "Truly?"

"Swear." Noemi replied with a grin. "Wanna see?"

She opened the passenger-side door and reached in for the sweet deliciousness.

Antonio could not resist. Even the day after it was baked, the aroma of cherries and pastry was unmistakable. He joined Angelo.

"Ok, you can share this… *after* you've listened to me. Deal?"

The two looked at each other, then at the crostata, then at Noemi, then back at each other. They nodded and replied in unison. "Deal."

Taking a steadying breath and praying she could find the words to convince them, Noemi started to speak. She talked for more than five minutes, but the two boys were riveted, and she was fairly certain, by the time she was halfway through her exposition they were sold on the idea.

"Lemme get this straight…" Antonio, the harder nut to crack, said when she wound up, "… all we 'ave to do is come with you, join your bunch of crazies, and help around the camp? What's in it for us? We got everything we need here and don't have to do anything."

"Safety." Noemi said.

"Rubbish," Angelo countered derisively. "No one's safe anymore."

"Fair enough," Noemi conceded. "So, how about a warm bed, regular food, and kids your own age who aren't trying to steal your ill-gotten gains or kill you?"

"Speaking of which, any idea where our food from yesterday went?" Angelo griped.

"Nearest rubbish bin I could find," Noemi replied, quashing the urge to laugh at their appalled expressions.

Angelo huffed, then nudged Antonio and jerked his head.

The pair walked out of Noemi's hearing range and a fierce discussion ensued. It was obvious to Noemi that Angelo wanted to take up her offer, while Antonio was suspicious of her intentions.

She understood his scepticism; doubtless their *status* in the neighbourhood was hard won, and equally hard to relinquish.

Noemi fought to hide a smile at the image of these two at the helm of the gangs prowling Trastevere.

Then again what do I actually know about them? Nothing. They could be cold-blooded killers.

Refusing to believe they would harm her, conveniently forgetting what happened at this very house scant nights ago, she quashed the notion and ignored the chill snaking down her spine.

"I'm not asking you to give up your independence, just be part of a group of like-minded people who don't need to fight for every scrap of food," she raised her voice slightly.

Antonio was grumbling darkly when, eventually, they trudged back to where Noemi was standing.

"I don't trust you, but Angelo wants to give it a try. My turn to make a deal."

Her expression giving nothing away, Noemi waited.

"We come for a protionary... probatty... probationary period." Antonio stumbled a little over the complex word. "Three months. If we like it, we'll stay, if not we'll come home... no questions asked."

The two boys fidgeted while Noemi appeared to consider their counteroffer. Inwardly, she was cheering. Outwardly, she dipped her head in formal acknowledgement.

"Deal." She held out her hand.

The three shook, and Noemi handed over the crostata.

By the time they had lived in the encampment for three weeks... never mind three months... neither Antonio nor Angelo had any intention of returning to the streets of Trastevere.

14

Ten Years Later

B y tradition — or was it duty, compassion, possibly guilt, whatever nebulous emotion tightened Noemi's gut — she watched another of their number being consumed by the flames.

No matter how many times Death visited their encampment, it never got easier for the woman who had, unofficially but inexorably, ended up in charge... acquiring, to her chagrin, the honorific of Padrona.

A weakness she would never reveal to anyone else, not even her daughters. She could not afford to.

For the last decade, they had wandered Italy, aimlessly, in search of a place to call their own. Whenever they attempted to establish a camp near a city, whispers of an old crone who practiced ancient magic began to circulate, of how she ensorcelled young and old alike into joining her flock and doing her bidding.

Nothing was further from the truth.

In the years following the plague, the number of qualified

medical professionals plummeted to near extinction. Any who sought treatment and refuge with Noemi, sent word to their kin of her capabilities.

Resentment among the officials of the various cities — unable to retain specialists of any discipline — increased in direct proportion to the caravan's numbers. Initial efforts by the camp leaders to negotiate a tentative truce resulted in the arrival of armed soldiers.

Each skirmish honed the skills of Noemi's clan and, under Santino's expert tutelage, everyone, no matter their age, learned to fight and kill.

The former soldier took his duty to protect the inhabitants of the camp seriously.

At first, they were no match, forced to retreat and regroup time and time again, leading to funeral pyres versus decent burials but, eventually and with dogged persistence, they gained the upper hand. Soon, they were the ones driving invaders from their lands.

Hatred for the Farmers and City Dwellers intensified until Noemi's clan eliminated any who dared cross them, decapitating the dead as a warning to others.

Somewhere along the way, a taxidermist and his boy joined the camp. The man possessed a strange penchant for preserving heads taken in battle and transforming them into war trophies which hung proudly on the walls of the victors.

They brought it on themselves, was Noemi's justification for the macabre custom.

Picking up a stick, she held it against the dying blaze until it ignited, and used it to light the cigarette she plucked from behind her ear.

She inhaled deeply, savouring the taste of the smoke for a moment, then tossed the twig back into the flames.

"I know what you're going to say," she addressed the

corpse. "Yes, it is a nasty habit and will eventually kill me, but does it really matter if it shortens my life?"

Cigarettes had become the unofficial coin in the Outlands. A carton could buy a good horse or two; a case got you a reasonably decent caravan. Even human life had its price, although it was much cheaper. A pack of cigarettes was all it cost for a night with a prostitute.

Finding them was like mining for gold. Even after all this time, stockpiles of the cancer sticks lay forgotten in abandoned stores and warehouses, waiting to be rediscovered, and much easier to transport than the heavy yellow metal.

If, occasionally, Noemi dipped into the encampment's supply, she chalked it up to payment for overseeing this odd clowder of cats.

Another deep puff triggered a racking cough, and a plume of smoke swirled skywards to merge with the billowing cloud from the pyre.

Tears streaked down Noemi's cheeks but, if anyone saw, she would blame the smoke.

Wiping her face with the back of her hand to rid herself of the unnecessary moisture, she bid the body a final farewell.

"For your sake, Santino, I pray paradise awaits you. I know we became your family, and that you loved us in your own way, even if we never overcame our individual grief. In all this senseless destruction, only you would find a way to die from a disease humanity thought it had defeated a long time ago. From where in God's name did you contract TB?"

Noemi took one last drag on her cigarette and tried to frame her thoughts.

"If you find Giulio and Chiara waiting for you, give them my regards and apologise to Giulio for not being able to spend eternity with him. If God does exist, I doubt He will let me into Heaven for what I have become."

Flicking the butt of her cigarette onto the pyre, Noemi turned to see Bianca and Sophia standing like silent sentinels in miniature, and cursed Santino for teaching her children how to stalk game without being heard.

Wordlessly, Noemi enveloped the girls in her arms and led them back to their caravan.

Santino's death prompted fifteen-year-old Nicoletta to draw in on herself. Unexpectedly orphaned, she felt no longer answerable to anyone but herself.

Noemi tried to rein her in, which only made matters worse, eliciting the inevitable and truculent contention that, "You are *not* my mother."

The teen had no problem convincing her younger friend to skip her studies and go hunting. If the pair got caught, Nicoletta feigned innocence and blamed the boys.

A state of affairs which continued until the day her shenanigans nearly cost Sophia and herself their lives.

It was close to midnight, and the camp was quiet when Nicoletta knocked on Sophia's window. Sophia popped the glass from its frame and scrambled to the ground.

"Are you sure we won't get into trouble for this, Nic?"

"You are such a worry wart." Nicoletta rolled her eyes in disgust. "We'll be back before anyone knows we're gone."

Under cover of darkness, the two girls crept from camp, and headed to an orchard, Nicoletta had come across quite by accident the last time she ran off after another argument with Noemi.

Half an hour's steady walking brought the pair to a fence which enclosed the apple trees.

Sophia studied the metallic barrier, guesstimating the top to be about three meters high. *How are we supposed to scale that?* "You dragged me out of bed for this?" She scowled. "There's no way we can climb it, so we might as well—"

"Shut up and watch," Nicoletta retorted in a hushed voice.

From her kit, she retrieved a pair of heavy-duty tin snips, then dropped onto her knees to cut the fence.

"Are they Dario's?" Sophia demanded incredulously, trying to come to terms with the fact that, on top of everything else, her friend was a thief. "He's been looking everywhere for them."

"Not my fault he's careless with his tools."

"Nicoletta Bernardi, you know he doesn't leave his tools scattered about. He was using them when they disappeared."

"So, I found them, and my need is greater than his," Nicoletta defended, snipping a hole large enough for them to slip through.

Once inside the orchard, Sophia had a change of heart. The sweet fragrance of the ripened Royal Gala apples, although subtle, was irresistible. Snatching one from the lowest branch of a nearby tree, she bit into its juicy flesh with a crunch.

"Dammit," Nicoletta hissed, "would you be quiet?"

"Why? It's the middle of the night. There's no one around. You said, yourself, we're safe here."

"You never know."

The two thought better of wasting time arguing and began to pick apples. Sophia concentrated on the lower hanging fruit, while Nicoletta climbed higher in search of what she believed to be fresher apples.

Clinging precariously onto a branch, she caught the flicker of something moving in the orchard. Seconds later, the sound of men's voices came within earshot.

"It's probably just some animal who wriggled under the fence."

"Then why do we have to bother looking?"

"Because it's what we get paid for."

"Still a pointless excer…" the second man trailed off, distracted by the sound of rustling leaves ahead of them.

"Get out of there, Nic, before you get caught." Sophia urged in a stage whisper.

The exhortation was followed by an, "Ooof", when Nicoletta jumped out of the tree, landing heavily, certain she had twisted her ankle.

As she rose to her feet, wincing in pain, two men, their clothing vaguely militaristic, materialised from the shadow of the trees, swords drawn.

"Well, now, what do we have here, Aldo?" the guard who appeared to be in charge asked.

"Looks like a couple of lost kitties," Aldo replied. "I bet they'll bring a pouch of nice shiny coins at auction."

"Aye, but not until we've had a little fun with them."

Armed only with their hunting knives, Sophia warned, "S-stay away, unless you want to d-die."

"Awww… do you hear that Emiliano," Aldo chuckled. "The kittens have claws."

"Adds to the fun." Emiliano licked his lips.

The two guards advanced, weapons at the ready.

Assuming the defensive stance her father had drilled into her, Nicoletta prepared to take on both, to save her friend. Sophia was having none of that and took her place beside Nicoletta.

The tension in the air was broken by the thud of boots approaching at a run from behind. Nicoletta spun around, ready to lash out at whoever was attempting to attack from their blind side.

Abject relief swept through her when she saw Dante brandishing his sword, and she turned to face the guards with renewed vigour.

"Get out of here, whelp. This has nothing to do with you," the one called Aldo ordered.

"No can do. These two belong to me," Dante said smugly as both girls glanced over their shoulders at him.

The men advanced on the trio.

The ensuing clash was furious.

Dante did his best to protect Nicoletta and Sophia from the onslaught who, in turn, slashed at the guards, determined to keep them off-balance.

Nicoletta's knife filleted one of their attackers whose blood sprayed everywhere as he crumpled to his knees, his blade falling to the ground.

Sophia blocked Emiliano's attempt to plunge his sword into Dante's chest when he reached down to snatch the discarded sword and toss it to Nicoletta.

Advancing on the second guard, Dante and Nicoletta cut him down quickly, but not before he fired a warning flare.

Drenched in blood, the trio's flight was delayed by Nicoletta who refused to leave without claiming their enemies' heads. They were earned in a fair fight, making them rightful trophies.

Reaching the opening in the fence, Dante went through first to check the field on the opposite side remained clear.

Sophia's tunic snagged on the barbed metal. The drum of booted feet heralding reinforcements compelled Dante to grab Sophia's arms and haul her through the hole while Nicoletta shoved from behind.

Later, they discovered the struggle had left Sophia with a deep laceration across her back. When it healed, the jagged scar became a permanent reminder of their frantic flight, and, despite the circumstances surrounding their escapade, cemented a burgeoning bond between the two girls.

Nicoletta never forgot that coaxing Sophia into her reckless capers might have ended in tragedy. Unbeknownst to either girl, *this* was the moment when Nicoletta's future as Sophia's best friend, protector, and right-hand woman was sealed — an indelible link, forged.

The three made it back to the outskirts of the camp before any of them spoke.

Panting from their headlong dash, Nicoletta asked Dante, "How did you know where we were?"

"Easy, I've been following you since you left camp. I'm on watch tonight, and you two did a lousy job of sneaking out."

Risking a solid left hook, he took a step closer to Nicoletta and enfolded her in his arms. "If you *ever* pull a stunt like that again, you'll answer to me."

"Is that supposed to scare me?" Nicoletta retaliated, unable… quite… to prevent the grin tilting her lips.

"It'll be more terrifying than what you two are about to face. Now, go get Sophia patched up before she bleeds out."

Greatly daring, he gave Nicoletta a quick kiss and headed back to his rounds.

Swallowing hard to quell the butterflies that were nothing to do with Noemi's wrath, Nicoletta helped Sophia to her mother's caravan.

15

The years ticked by; the seasons changed and, slowly, life settled into a rhythm. Far removed from the life anyone, whether they be city folk or nomads, had known before, but a rhythm all the same.

As Noemi's company expanded, several decided to go their separate ways, preferring the cooler climes further north, or the fertile slopes of the balmy southern regions. Communication between the disparate groups was sporadic, but updates filtered through.

Rumours about these so-called land-walkers ranged from the sublime to the ridiculous. Some claimed they were murderous lunatics who practised cannibalism. Others alleged the virus had caused terrible mutations leaving them resembling wild animals, or they had become giants who scaled city walls with ease in the hunt for their prey… which they tore limb from limb.

Although, initially, far from the truth, the nomadic tribes roaming the peninsula… and possibly elsewhere in Europe… refused to conform to the new world order. Their aversion to the inhabitants of the cities, kindled when the virus was running rampant, and strengthened when their very existence was threatened, solidified into an implacable hatred.

All too soon, the land-walkers, decreed to be villains by their *civilised* counterparts, bore a new label — The Hunters. Their killing sprees became the stuff of legends, and of nightmares. Any parent who wanted their children to behave only had to mention The Hunters, and their offspring transformed into angelic cherubs instantly.

Conversely, the city-folk gravitated towards nurturing society instead of eliminating it. In the decades since the pandemic they had, by trial and error, learnt to cultivate the land by hand, as had their ancestors. They established enclaves in what remained of the cities around the world… living cheek by jowl with those The Hunters deemed less… *competent.*

They became known as The Dwellers.

History would record that the virus, combined with unproven antidotes had resulted in a hodgepodge of genetic anomalies, which manifested in a variety of unexpected… and unorthodox… ways.

None of this was any consolation to a fledgeling society who had already allowed fear to divide them… almost irrevocably.

Noemi, Rome never far from her mind, was drawn back to the outskirts of her erstwhile home. Unwilling to venture too close to the capital, more because the confines of city life held no appeal than in fear of reprisals from the Dwellers, Noemi assumed dominion over the central band of Italy.

In loose terms, this included the regions of Abruzzo, Lazio, Umbria, Marche and lower Tuscany. Regions, once renowned for their diverse cultures, rich heritage, and arresting landscapes, were now deserted, leaving nature to assume control.

To Noemi, it was as though this land had lain dormant awaiting the arrival of her rag-tag posse of outcasts who, weary of wandering, were desperate to put down roots. A land where they could thrive, as long as they were prepared to work hard.

There was no one to contest her claim.

For a time… contingent upon the Hunters and the Dwellers steering clear of each other, tensions between the foes did not abate as much as ease… albeit marginally. It seemed unlikely a truce could ever be forged, let alone a peace, but the decline in the number of dead bodies was enough to engender a sense of normality… however ephemeral.

Skirmishes were inevitable and the Hunters rarely lost an encounter, accumulating a ghoulish assortment of heads, several of which were displayed… on a rotating basis… around the perimeter of the encampment in warning to any passing traveller who fancied issuing a challenge.

Life was a struggle, yet, despite the odds stacked against them, the Hunters were determined to survive.

Until the year a bitter snowstorm threatened to finish what the pandemic had started.

The mild winter temperatures normally associated with the lower regions of Italy had been supplanted by an arctic blast from the northern Alps. Instead of refreshing rain, deep snow blanketed the earth, reminding those who could recall a time before the pandemic of Christmas cards.

While the freezing weather proved an obstacle for the Dwellers, the Hunters excelled in these conditions. Wild animals such as boar and deer were easier to follow as they foraged for their own sources of food.

The youngsters, including Sophia and Nicoletta, revelled in the thrill of the chase, honing their skills in the art of tracking, stalking, and pursuing, as they roamed the countryside with the experienced members of the encampment.

Except Bianca.

Bianca had no desire to hunt. It was not that she was any less proficient than her peers but preferred to spend her time buried in her mother's medical tomes, predisposed to sustaining rather than ending life.

That Noemi's firstborn showed some interest in following her footsteps was one thing, but Bianca's staunch refusal to accept the other responsibilities associated with being Padrona of the camp was a whole other matter.

Stomping the snow off her boots, Bianca hung her bow and quiver on what was, in a previous existence, a hatrack. Empty-handed, she held her breath in anticipation of her mother's admonishment.

She did not have to wait long.

Arms folded, a half-smoked cigarette between her lips, Noemi remonstrated, "Your sister beat you again?"

"How the hell should I know?" Bianca snapped. "The six of them hunt like a pack of wolves, driving away any prey they haven't killed."

"It's up to you to get there first. *You* should be the one setting the example, leading the hunt, not playing catch up. You're the eldest and I need to know that when I decide to step—"

"Oh God, would you stop that. How many times have I told you? I Do Not Want To Be *You*! At least, not the way you are now." Bianca flicked her hand at the shrivelled heads on the wall. "You even have Sophia looking for any chance to collect one of those grotesque trophies."

"Enough," Noemi barked. "*You've* racked up your fair share."

"Doesn't mean I enjoyed the exercise. I want to be you *before* all the bloodshed. The woman who spent all those hours trying to protect humanity."

Stifling a sigh, Noemi tried to calm her emotions, to explain the facts of life to her oldest daughter. "As much as I would love to promise a future like that awaits you, it doesn't. I need to know you are capable of doing **both**. Sophia is not mature enough to assume the mantle, and I sure as hell can't depend on any of the boys, or Nicoletta."

"Why not Nic?" Bianca's tone was incredulous.

"We both know how hot-headed and impetuous she can be. Sophia's scars are proof enough."

"Come on, Mother," Bianca scoffed. "That was years ago. Nic's pledged her life to make sure danger does not find your youngest. You know how hard she's worked to turn herself around. Nic is one of the most trustworthy and dependable people in this camp. I cannot think of anyone *more* deserving of the responsibility. She's family too."

While Noemi could not deny this, she was not prepared to let Bianca off the hook.

"I do not disagree, but…" she raised her palm to cut off Bianca's counter-argument, "that does not mean you get to shirk your duties."

Resentment reared its ugly head, and Bianca gaped at her mother. "Duties? Is that all I am to you, someone to do your bidding? I am your daughter, not some random Hunter."

"Bianca—"

"I'm sorry, I'm not who you want me to be. Do you even care about my feelings? I'm sick of trying to please you, trying to be someone I'm not." Bianca heard how over-dramatic she sounded, but she was tired, and reason had taken a holiday.

"D'you know what? I wish someone would whisk me away from this living nightmare, this insanity you call a family, to care for me the way you tell us Papa cared for you, a sentiment I would a reciprocate a thousand percent."

Noemi threw up her hands in disgust. "Stop with your delusions, Bianca, and do as I instructed. There's plenty of daylight left. Take your damned bow and bring back food. I do not care whether it's a boar or a rabbit. Anything to prove to me, and the rest of camp, that you possess the skills and guts to take care of those who depend on us—"

Livid, Bianca yanked her bow and quiver off the rack, which clattered to the floor, and stormed out of the caravan, leaving an equally infuriated Noemi to carp, "—and not just give up."

To prove Bianca's point, the game hunted by her sister and their five friends had fled, driven south in the direction of the city Noemi had forbidden any to approach on their own.

The day wore on; the wind grew colder, and the gunmetal grey of the heavily laden clouds warned a savage storm was in the offing.

Under normal circumstances, Bianca bore a healthy respect for the weather and knew how quickly it could turn at this time of the year. Perversely, today, she ignored the alarm bells clanging in her head and refused to quit, determined to return home with something for the pot.

After trudging for what felt like hours, and on the verge of admitting defeat, she stumbled upon a set of what appeared to be recent deer tracks.

Five more minutes, she groused inwardly, *then I'm going home, sod the bloody stag.* Straightening weary shoulders, she followed the trail into an unsheltered expanse of open pasture. The breeze picked up, whining through the trees bordering the field. There was a sour edge to the air, and snowflakes were spiralling down from the darkening sky in a lazy dance.

Prudence dictated she turn tail and make a run for it but, in that split-second of vacillation, the temperature plummeted, the wind increased to a wild howl, and the gentle veil of white deteriorated into a dizzying blizzard.

Almost before Bianca could blink, all tracks... her own and those of the game she was hunting... were obliterated. Desperate efforts to orient herself were in vain, her sense of direction lost.

The snow accumulated faster than Bianca could move. A creeping cold threatened, numbing her fingers. She slung her bow over her shoulder and thrust her hands into her coat pockets.

Aware of how rapidly hypothermia could overtake a

person, Bianca sank to her knees to build a snow shelter the way Santino had taught her.

Using her hands, she shovelled the snow into a large heap. Mindful of Santino's instructions, Bianca ensured it was dome-shaped, so the sides supported the weight of the roof.

Every so often, she packed down the snow to reduce the chance of the shelter collapsing when she hollowed it out.

Mixing older drifts with the freshly fallen powder, she let the snow harden.

Exhaustion was setting in, and she feared frostbite would claim her fingers.

Switching from her hands to her bow, she dug a hole into the mound to remove as much from the inside as she dared.

She remembered the most important thing Santino had taught her about building a snow shelter — leave a hole about fifteen centimetres in diameter at the top of the shelter to allow carbon dioxide to escape.

Worming her way inside, she collapsed.

Before Bianca could seal the entrance, she lost consciousness.

16

The arctic blast did not abate.

Noemi paced her caravan, expecting Bianca to appear through the door at any second, but it was a wasted vigil.

She could not believe she had allowed her temper to get the better of her. Sending her daughter out into the deteriorating afternoon smacked of petulance, but she had expected Bianca to return hours before the storm hit, brandishing her kill with her usual sass.

Hell, even an inebriated squirrel can find an acorn.

A loud pounding penetrated her grim thoughts. She raced to the door and, yanking it open, exclaimed, "Bianca, thank heavens you're safe."

Her eyes adjusted to the early morning darkness, recognising Antonio and Dante, caked in snow, icy breath frozen to their scarves.

They glanced at each other, seemingly at a loss for words.

"What?" Noemi demanded.

"Padrona," Antonio began. "We have searched as far as we dare and can find no trace of Bianca."

His eyes glittered as the tears he refused to let fall froze on his lashes. "I am so sorry."

"Thank you for trying. Go, get yourselves dry," Noemi replied, the smile she summoned up devoid of warmth, and shut the door before they could respond.

Crumpling to the floor, she wrapped her arms around her knees and began to rock, weeping for her loss and begging forgiveness from Bianca's spirit for failing her as a mother.

Bianca stretched and yawned.

She was no longer cold. Her fingers brushed against what felt like a heavy woollen blanket, which carried a scent she did not recognise.

Her eyes flew open, and she squinted to focus on her surroundings.

Am I hallucinating? Worse, am I dead? Maybe this blanket is not wool, but the collapsed roof of my snow cave and I'm buried. Is this what hypothermia feels like? Is this the afterlife? Questions raced through her mind.

Her hands roamed across her body, to discover she was dry, and not dressed in her soaked clothing. In fact, she was wearing a well-worn, but beautifully made, oversized, cotton nightshirt.

The thud of footsteps broke the hush. Bianca's senses went on high alert, and her gaze swivelled in the direction of the sound. Instinctively, she reached for her knife, which was not there.

A giant of a man entered the room.

In a gruff but cheery voice, he greeted, "I'm pleased to see you have woken. When I found you in my field, I was afraid it was too late. You were wise to place that bow by your shelter's entrance. Wouldn't have noticed it otherwise."

He bent to lift a plate from a bedside table, replacing it with another. The inviting aroma of freshly cooked food tickled Bianca's nostrils and her stomach rumbled. Logic told her to be suspicious; emotion was too hungry to care. Shifting on the bed, she looked at the platter wistfully, but did not move.

Following her gaze, the man explained, "I have no clue how long you were out there, but I figured offering you several smaller morsels was better for your stomach. Is there anything else I can get you?"

Mutely, Bianca shook her head. Tentatively, she reached for a slice of toasted ciabatta, and bit into its buttery goodness, savouring the taste.

Her host… *kidnapper?*… smiled at her attempt to eat and poured her a cup of lemon tea.

Interpreting her wary expression correctly, he drained the cup in one gulp then poured another in the same cup.

Death of trust at the hands of the plague had saddened the man.

Bianca took a sip, letting the fragrant liquid glide down her parched throat, soothing and refreshing. Gathering enough strength, she croaked, "How long?"

"Have you been asleep?" the man finished her question. "About three days. Like I said, I was concerned you might never regain consciousness. It took me a while to massage the colour back into your fingers."

He swallowed a guffaw at the shock on her face.

"I'm sorry I did not beg your permission to touch you, but you were dead to the world and time was of the essence."

Nodding her understanding, she pointed to herself and rasped, "Bianca."

Her host patted his chest. "A pleasure to meet you, Bianca, I am Gabriel."

You can follow the adventures of Gabriel, Bianca, and their friends in…
Echoes and Illusions
The Hunters: Book One.

RORI BLEU

With a smattering of riverboat pirates and royalty in her heritage, Rori Bleu's childhood reflected her past. An interest in fairy tales, myth and legend were as important as spirited discussions around politics and current affairs — although some might argue they are one and the same!

A fascination, sparked by listening to Grimm's Fairy Tales at her grandmother's knee, not only encouraged Rori's passion for reading, but also steered her into the world of RPG's. What began as a fun pastime, soon evolved into the creation of fantastical worlds, but Rori never lost her love of politics going on to specialise in Governmental History and Historical Research.

Naturally this means her stories are steeped in historical accuracy and real-life intrigue. While Rori's love of a happily ever after means her preferred genre is romance, don't be surprised if you discover an occasional detour into historical fiction, thrillers, horror and fantasy.

ROSIE CHAPEL

Rosie Chapel lives in Perth, Australia with her hubby and very spoilt rescue dog. When not writing, she loves catching up with friends, burying herself in a book (or three), discovering the wonders of Western Australia, or — and the best — a quiet evening at home with her husband, enjoying a glass of wine and a movie.

Website: www.rosiechapel.com

ALSO BY RORI BLEU

Pineapple Meringue

Imprisoned Hearts

Port of London

Dani's Masquerade

Black Tulips

Ajei's Destiny

Porta Aeternum

The Queen's Heart

Syn *with Matthew Forester*

*****

With Rosie Chapel

Echoes and Illusions - The Hunters: Book 1

Smoke and Mirrors - The Hunters: Book 2

Evie's War

Vindicta

Corrupt Covenant

Lesser of Two Evils

Deadly Incision

The Sela Helsdatter Saga

A Flip of The Coin - Book One

Conceived Chaos - Book Two

Odin's Bane - Book Three

Valhalla's Doom - Book Four

Arcane Alchemy: Freya's Fate - *A Helsdatter Saga Novella*

ALSO BY ROSIE CHAPEL

<u>Historical Fiction</u>

The Hannah's Heirloom Sequence
The Pomegranate Tree - Book One
Echoes of Stone and Fire - Book Two
Embers of Destiny - Book Three
Etched in Starlight - Prequel
Hannah's Heirloom Trilogy - Compilation — e-book only

Prelude to Fate
Legacy of Flame and Ash

The Nettleby Trilogy (WW1 Novellas)
A Guardian Unexpected - Book One
Under the Clock - Book Two
Between Heartbeats - Book Three

<u>Regency Romances</u>
The Linen and Lace Series
Once Upon An Earl - Book One
To Unlock Her Heart - Book Two
Love on a Winter's Tide - Book Three
A Love Unquenchable - Book Four
A Hidden Rose — Book Five

An Unexpected Romance
Elusive Hearts - Book One

Shrouded Hearts - Book Two

The Daffodil Garden

The Unconventional Duchess

Rescuing Her Knight - *the de Wiltons:* Book One

His Fiery Hoyden

A Regency Duet

A Regency Christmas Double

Fate is Curious

A Christmas Prayer *with Ashlee Shades*

The Lady's Wager

Winning Emma

A Love Impossible

Unravelling Roana

Love Kindled

Moonbeams and Mistletoe

<u>Fairy Tale Romance</u>

Chasing Bluebells

<u>Contemporary Romances</u>

Of Ruins and Romance

All At Once It's You

Cobweb Dreams

Just One Step

His Heart's Second Sigh

*****

<u>With Rori Bleu</u>

Echoes and Illusions - The Hunters: Book 1

Smoke and Mirrors - The Hunters: Book 2

Evie's War

Vindicta

Corrupt Covenant

Lesser of Two Evils

Deadly Incision

The Sela Helsdatter Saga

A Flip of The Coin - Book One

Conceived Chaos - Book Two

Odin's Bane - Book Three

Valhalla's Doom - Book Four

Arcane Alchemy: Freya's Fate - *A Helsdatter Saga Novella*